The author was born and bred in Glasgow, Scotland in 1965. He has a degree in Journalism and enjoys music, travelling and writing.

Gerard and Sawkins

HAIZEAN

AUSTIN MACAULEY PUBLISHERS™

LONDON * CAMBRIDGE * NEW YORK * SHARJAH

A CIP catalogue record for this title is available from the British Library.

ISBN 9781035858736 (Paperback)
ISBN 9781035858743 (ePub e-book)

www.austinmacauley.com

First Published 2024
Austin Macauley Publishers Ltd®
1 Canada Square
Canary Wharf
London
E14 5AA

Introduction

The novel is about family, friendships, war, peace, history, hope, endurance and ultimately reconciliation. It is about stopping for a moment and seeing the world from another person's point of view in different times, cultures, and environments. The first part of the book centres around two small, yet significant villages, Scotstoun, Glasgow and Guernica in the Basque region, northern Spain. Set before, during and after World War II, it should be noted that two of the main characters include a doctor and nurse at a time when there was no NHS.

The second part of the book focuses on a Peace Centre set up in a flat in Scotstoun called Haizean (Basque for in the wind), where students come from all over the world to share ideas.

"The bombing of Guernica, eighty-five years ago, inspired one of Picasso's best-known works. Now, visitors to this iconic part of Spain's Basque Country will discover a town devoted to peace and reconciliation. It is also about using art as a form of protest to encourage change and make people think objectively, rather than react irrationally."

James Gerard

Imagine living in enforced exile for nearly forty years of your life. Add to that the lack of any of your fellow-countrymen within a thousand miles. Asier was a doctor living in Guernica back in 1937 alongside his wife and two children when the German bombers arrived. He has to assume that his family have all perished. Arriving in Glasgow, thanks to the efforts of John Oswald, a Scottish journalist, Asier carries on his work as a doctor.

Asier's diaries afford some insight into his coming to terms with separation from his homeland, namely' the Basque region in the north of Spain. But more than this, they chronicle key events leading up to, during and after World War II.

Background

John Sawkins

Spain, 1936

After two years of right-wing government, a Popular Front coalition of left-wing and liberal parties narrowly wins parliamentary elections and seeks to reintroduce the radical policies of 1931. A coup by right-wing military leaders captures only part of the country, leading to three years of civil war.

Nazi Germany and Fascist Italy actively support the nationalist rebels, whilst only the Soviet Union provides highly conditional assistance to the Republic. Britain and France support an arms embargo that effectively dooms the Republic, despite enthusiastic volunteers from all over Europe and the Americas who join the Communist-run International Brigades.

1939

General Francisco Franco leads the Nationalists to victory in the Civil War. More than 350,000 Spaniards died in the fighting, and Franco purges all remaining Republicans. Spain remains neutral throughout World War II, although the government's sympathies clearly lie with the Axis powers. The fighting displaced millions of Spaniards. Some 500,000 refugees fled in 1939 to France, where many of them would be interned in camps. 15,000 Spanish Republicans ended up in Nazi concentration camps after 1940.

Guernica

Guernica is a mural-sized oil painting on canvas by Spanish artist Pablo Picasso. The painting, which uses a palette of grey, black, and white, is known as one of the most moving and powerful anti-war paintings in history. Standing at 3.49 metres (11 ft 5 in) tall and 7.76 metres (25 ft 6 in) wide, the large mural shows the suffering of people, animals, and buildings wrenched by violence and chaos.

The painting was a response to the bombing of Guernica, a Basque village in northern Spain, by German and Italian warplanes at the request of the Spanish Nationalists. The bombing is considered one of the first raids in the history of modern military aviation on a defenceless civilian population.

"The Spanish Civil War gave me an opportunity to put my young air force to the test, and a means for my men to gain experience."

German Air Chief Hermann Göring testified at his trial after World War II: Some of these experimental tactics were tested on that bright spring day with devastating results—the Basque market town of Guernica was destroyed with a loss of life estimated at 1,650.

Upon completion, *Guernica* was displayed around the world in a brief tour, becoming famous and widely acclaimed, and helped to bring worldwide attention to the Spanish Civil War.

Ancient Basque Tree, Guernica

Information About the Basques

The Basques are an ancient race who have survived for thousands of years in an area situated to the north of Spain as well as in the south of France, though the majority (approx. 2.5 million) do live in Spain. The survival of the people and their unique language is all the more remarkable after domination from so many other invaders, including the Romans, the Visigoths, the Arabs, the French and the Spanish, not to mention Gascons and Catalans.

Perhaps inevitably over that time successive oppressors have sought to undermine the Basque autonomy by forbidding them from speaking their native tongue. (Similar methods were employed, for example, by the Russians in Lithuania; the Gaelic language was similarly targeted by the British; children would suffer corporal punishment for not speaking English).

There are now Basque television stations, dedicated to promoting all things Basque, but crucially the Basque language. (*Euskera*, is a so-called isolate, having no apparent remaining links with other European languages). As there are no similarities whatsoever with English, this makes learning to speak Basque a very difficult task (According to folklore, the devil himself gave up trying after seven years!).

The Basques had no tradition of using a written form of the language, even as late as the 19th century. Again, it could be that an oral tradition enabled the Basque language to survive. There remain the *bertsolariak* who are traditional singers as well as storytellers. Their role seems to be like that of the medieval troubadours.

Perhaps the tenacity with which Basques have clung on is down to preserving rituals, dances and traditions, such as the running of bulls in Pamplona. Basque men preserve the tradition of wearing a flat wide black beret. The game of *pelote* is very popular with the Basques.

One long-standing tradition has been for the community to gather for meetings beneath an oak tree. The 'Tree of Guernica' reinforces a sense of community, and the notion continues to this day, as successive oak trees replace their predecessors. Crucially, the Tree of Guernica survived the bombing of Guernica by the Germans in 1937.

In the aftermath of this horrific event, the British found some compassion, taking some of the orphaned children into their homes in Hampshire. Much like today with the children surviving in the Calais 'Jungle', the British government were rather reluctant to encourage the resettlement of other nationalities in Britain and even contemplated repatriating them upon their arrival, but local people were prepared to be far more welcoming.

Whether the clothing given them by Marks and Spencer, or the chocolate donated by Cadbury's was just a publicity stunt is unclear. Perhaps firms were prepared to be genuinely altruistic in those days. Equally, the Basques have a strong Catholic faith, and indeed, St Ignatius Loyola, the founder of the Jesuit order, was himself a Basque. Many devout Basques will walk the long pilgrimage along the Camino de Santiago de Compostela which is marked out by a line of yellow symbols in the shape of shells.

The *Katcha-Ranka* is a dance performed in fishing villages, where someone representing Saint Peter is carried in a coffin through the village and down to the sea. The dancers pretend to beat him as this portends a good catch. (St. Peter was himself a fisherman.) *Pastorales* are traditional Basque plays that are frequently performed, somewhat akin to medieval mystery plays.

The church is a powerful institution, as is the family. Neither of these has ever been successfully undermined by the state. There is a strong tradition of community in *Euskadi*, the Basque nation. The nearest neighbour, *lehen auzo*, has a key role in this. He (or she) can look after the farm during a family emergency. Additionally, it is from this neighbouring family that the best man and matron of honour are chosen when a wedding approaches.

Women have always experienced greater equality in Basque society. They too can inherit the family farm. Whilst the nuclear family is quite usual in cities, in rural areas, there is generally an extended family, with grandparents and children having a role to play in helping to manage the farm, as well as sundry maiden aunts and uncles. These relatives can all fulfil a role in the upbringing of children; it is not just the parents' job.

There is a long tradition of men moving herds of sheep, cows and goats up to the mountain pastures during the summer, whilst their womenfolk take charge of the farms back home. It is not uncommon for cousins to marry. Though this may help to ensure the Basque race remains pure, from a purely genetic perspective, exogenesis would have been a far healthier option. Examining the blood types locally, it is apparent that such customs persisted from a time long before other European groups appeared on the scene.

Not all the Basque Country is rural, of course, and Bilbao represents a shining example of the industry at its peak, with cars and machine tools featuring alongside shipbuilding.

Though *Euskadi* has gained a degree of control over its affairs since the death of Franco in 1975, there is still a resistance movement that continues to perpetrate violent acts with a view to gaining greater autonomy. *Euskadi Ta Askatasuna*, or ETA, fights for liberty and a true Basque homeland, though explosions tend to be confined to the Spanish regions alone: the *Pays Basques* in France, however, do help, as well as provide safe havens for their compatriots on the Spanish side of the border.

In Vitoria-Gasteiz, one can see banners suspended from windows, saying: EUSKAL PRESO ETA IHESLARIAK ETXERA. This highlights the additional punishment placed on the terrorists' relatives, since prisoners will often be located hundreds of miles away from their families. Today, children are taught the Basque language in schools.

Basque people are passionate about football with most supporting Athletico-Bilbao.

Scotstoun, Glasgow

Scotstoun was, until the early 1860s, the site of the Oswald family estate, which was centred on Scotstoun House.

By 1861, the westward expansion of the Clyde shipbuilding yards had reached Scotstoun with the opening of the Charles Connell and Company shipyard in 1861 and the new Yarrow Shipbuilders yard in 1906. This led to the break-up of the estate, as portions were sold off for housing, to create Victoria Park and for further industrial development (iron, engineering, and shipbuilding) along the river, with companies such as the Coventry Ordnance Works and Albion Motors locating in the area.

The southern part of Scotstoun is characterised by late 19th/ early 20th century tenements, whilst at its heart, and dating from a similar period, is a grid-like estate of mainly terraced cottage-style villas with distinctive English styling in wide tree-lined streets, an early example of Ebenezer Howard-type garden suburb town planning.

Scotstoun's Peace Tree, Victoria Park

The last member of the Oswald dynasty was James William Gordon Oswald. Before he died, he set up a trust fund for the care and education of orphans. The first ones to benefit from this were John and Ashlin Ritchie whose parents died in a horrific tram accident.

They were initially placed in a children's home in nearby Broomhill. They both worked hard and showed academic ability beyond their years. It was at this point they were placed in an Oswald property on Victoria Park Drive North. Over time, they inherited the property and the Oswald name.

Scotstoun house finished its days as a day nursery for toddlers and was demolished to make way for the present blocks of flats, at Kingsway Court, built in 1962 by Wimpey.

Today, Scotstoun has its own sports stadium, home to the Glasgow Warriors rugby union, and a world-class sports centre.

Glaswegians are also fanatical about football with most supporting the Old Firm, Celtic and Rangers.

Elizabeth Oswald, born in Scotstoun in 1767, lived in Scotstoun all her life. She followed the family tradition of carrying out charitable works and it was said that at ninety, she never seen a doctor, and at ninety-five, she still retained all her powers of mind and body. She is an inspiration to us all.

Our three heroes, Asier, Ashlin and John did not have the advantage of modern-day hospitals, technology, and medicines, so they used what they had. They focussed on all aspects of health—mental, physical, social, spiritual, and emotional well-being.

They made good use of Victoria Park (which came to be known as a place of healing). They made time for people to come and talk about their problems. They used music and social events to keep spirits up. At every opportunity, they would highlight the squalor their patients were living in. And their new surgery employed doctors, a nurse, a psychologist, and trainee doctors with the intention of tailor-making every individual's health care.

New technology has now allowed the surgery to link up with outside agencies; providing stress management, mental health self-management, massage, drop-in centres, money management, and all NHS services, in an effort to empower patients.

The three war heroes Ashlin, Asier and John, all met before the war in Glasgow. Asier was a visiting consultant from Spain at the Western Infirmary and met Ashlin who worked there as a nurse. She invited him back to dinner to meet John and somehow, they all just clicked. They spent many hours together discussing the differences between their countries. John and Asier cycled to Loch

Lomond and nearby beauty spots. The trio also made good use of Victoria Park, going on frequent walks and sitting on park benches, talking for hours.

"In Spain, we have benches on the streets. There is always time to talk," said Asier.

"Men talk, or as we say *blether*, on street corners here," said John.

"Women are too busy. We have to combine blethering with washing clothes in wash houses and doing all sorts of things," added Ashlin.

When Asier returned to Spain, the three kept in touch with letters, parcels and postcards.

Asier, Ashlin, and John listening to the radio in Scotstoun, 1935

The entertainment industry during World War II underwent changes to help aid the cause of the war. The entertainment industry during this time was often controlled by a country's government. Since the governments believed that a supportive home front was crucial to their countries' victory, they generally sought to keep the civilian spirits high and to depict the war in a positive light. With this motive in mind, governments engaged in the regulation and censorship of the forms of media, as well as the introduction of new methods of informing citizens through these media outlets.

Government censorship of mass media was enforced in much of the world during this time in fear of threatening the domestic harmony of a nation. Some of the most popular forms of entertainment during World War II were radio, film, and music. In conjunction with one another, these forms of media kept citizens entertained with a pastime, informed about their country's war efforts, and motivated them to contribute to the war effort.

Amigos

John Oswald's Diary, 1937

One morning, I received a letter from Asier asking me to come to Spain to witness the rise of Fascism and alert our government to the goings on in his country. Newspapers held a monopoly back then. The emerging BBC was not allowed to broadcast news until after 6pm.

I discussed the trip with my editor, spoke to some sympathisers, then made plans to travel. Any fears I had were far outweighed by the excitement of travelling abroad for the first time. I jumped at the chance. As well as meeting Asier's family and finding out all about their culture, I wanted to know exactly what was happening on mainland Europe at that time. The reports we were getting were patchy at best, and as my editor put it, "The first thing to go during wars is truth." It was getting in and out safely that concerned Ashlin.

"Don't be fooled. Killers are the same as you and I, except in different circumstances. Spain is a very dangerous place for journalists right now," she said.

"I promise. I won't tell a soul," I replied.

Travelling light, I made my way to Portsmouth by train. I took lodgings by the docks and visited a few bars frequented by fishermen. It was then I first met Seamus, whose every second word was 'fuck', or 'fuck off'. He still fished regularly in the Bay of Biscay and told me he would take me close to the mainland and I could row the rest of the way.

He then told me his fee was £500 to which I replied, "Fuck off." After an hour of heavy drinking, we settled on £200 with a rowing boat thrown in.

Seamus was, well, Irish; a master at his craft with the gift of the gab. He also liked a wee drink. On boarding the boat, he insisted on £100 up front. He then told me to get my head down and we would be there in the morning. I did and we were. Seamus even told me where to land, how to hide the boat, and how to get to Guernica.

"How do you know all of this?" I said.

"I'm not telling you," he replied.

"Would you like to give me an interview?" I said.

"Fuck off. Now on your way," was his reply. The Irishman's tips were a godsend and I reached Guernica in no time. Everyone knew each other and it wasn't long before I found Asier; my knowledge of Spanish and Latin helped too.

"John, you are here. I can't believe it. Come and meet my family," said Asier. Asier had a beautiful wife, Naiara. And two beautiful children Aitor, my son, and Agurtzane, my daughter. I was given a room with a single bed, a wardrobe, a small table and a chair. The window was open and the first thing that hit me was the pungent smell of rosemary and lavender. After I had a wash, Asier and I sat on the porch whilst Naiara made dinner.

"This is like Victoria Park with sunshine," I remarked.

"Well, John, if I could, I would take my family to Scotland right now. Our country is at war. And Fascism is spreading all over Europe. War is madness. As a doctor, a father, and human being, I'm lost," he replied.

"Is it safe for me to stay a while?" I said.

"Yes. Just wear my clothes, don't speak English and whatever you do, don't tell anyone you are a journalist," he replied.

That night, his wife prepared a feast fit for a king. "Most of our food comes from our garden. And we make our own wine," said Asier. We sat around the dinner table for more than two hours. Then Asier and I took turns on his guitar and sang songs. Asier and I rounded the night off on the porch smoking cigars and polishing off another bottle of wine. The next few weeks were spent reading newspapers, getting to know the area and trying to judge the threat of all-out war in Europe.

On Monday, 26 April 1937, Asier decided to take me fishing in the mountains. It was market day. People from the surrounding hillsides traditionally came together. His wife said she would take the kids, who were both excited as there was a rumour going around that sweets would be back on sale. The sun was shining and it seemed like it was a good day for almost anything.

On the way to Asier's favourite pool, we passed a young Italian priest sitting at a viewpoint over Guernica. He had a big bag full of what looked like flares. He also had a gun. "Great day to be out of Guernica," he said. We both just nodded and moved on. I could see that this comment bothered Asier. When we reached Asier's spot, we set up fishing poles and had lunch.

"What did that bastard mean?" Asier said. Everyone was on edge. What happened next would change the world forever. The church bells of Santa Maria sounded the alarm.

German bombers appeared in the skies over Guernica and immediately transformed the sleepy Spanish market town into an everlasting symbol of the atrocity of war. Unbeknown to the residents of Guernica, they had been slated by their attackers to become guinea pigs in an experiment designed to determine just what it would take to carpet bomb a city into oblivion.

We made our way down the mountain passing the young priest again. He smiled at us, and said, "That should do it."

Asier walked straight up to him and said, "Forgive me Lord for what I'm about to do," and shot him. I didn't even know he had a gun.

"Asier, you have just shot a priest," I cried.

"Believe me, John, he was no priest. And it was no coincidence that he was out of town today," he replied. We made our way off the mountain as quickly as possible.

When we reached the town, all that was left was smouldering rubble and the stench of dead bodies. The town as we knew it was no more. People trying to escape had been shot to pieces. We searched for hours for Asier's wife and children, stopping to help those who could be saved. Late that night, we returned to Asier's home, which was on the edge of town and was luckily still standing. There was no sign of his family anywhere.

We searched for two more days. One neighbour told us they didn't make it. Asier was shattered. He had patched up hundreds of patients and now faced his own pain.

Bombing of Guernica. The bombing of Guernica (26 April 1937) was an aerial carpet bombing of the Basque town of Guernica during the Spanish Civil War.

On the night of 28 April, I decided the best course of action would be to head to the coast with Asier and make our way to London.

I readied all we would need, then tried to numb Asier's pain with wine. After four bottles, he walked into the middle of his garden, knelt under a tree and cocked his pistol. "*Adios,* James. I just can't go on," said Asier. I had seen that look before. He meant it. Ashlin would have known what to do. I didn't. I was just an ordinary hack, out of my depth.

"Can I kiss you before you die?" I said.

"Of course," he replied.

I knelt beside him, cocked my head, and gave him the hardest Glasgow kiss (head butt) I could manage. He fell to the ground and I took his gun from him. The horse and cart were packed. I bundled him in and we headed for the coast. I then put him in the boat I had hidden and rowed as fast I could out to sea knowing British boats still fished in the Bay of Biscay.

After about two hours, we were picked up by Seamus. This was no coincidence. There was another man on the boat who seemed to know all about me. He said that he found my work interesting and that he was a British government agent.

After a thorough debriefing, he instructed me to travel to Scotstoun and ask Asier and Ashlin to set up a surgery to service the shipyards. He said he would forward all documents required for Asier. He also told me not to write about Guernica on a national basis, as they had a man doing this. Apparently, it would be alright to write about my trip in the Clydebank Press. Oddly, he told me to take Catholic lessons on how to say mass, funerals, christenings, and weddings. "We know your friend, Father George Gillespie, will help you. And we may need your expertise in Spanish at some point," he said.

Asier woke up with a sore head in Portsmouth and we made our way by train to Scotstoun.

3 Letting Go War Diaries

Ashlin, 1937

I encouraged Asier to write a letter back home as a way of dealing with his grief. I also encouraged him to keep a diary.

Asier: a letter to my family, my homeland and my culture. Scotstoun, 1937.

My dearest family and friends,

I write to you with a heavy heart. Words cannot express the sense of loss that I have experienced, but I feel I must express my thoughts and emotions in writing, if only to exorcise the crushing effect they are having on my soul, as they race around in a seemingly interminable loop, revisiting the trauma of all that carnage.

But above all, I cannot bear to have to come to terms with the fact that my wife has gone: taken from me in the Glasgow way. Equally painful is the realisation that both my son and daughter have similarly had their lives snuffed out; lives that promised so much. It's worse when children die. This should not be. They were supposed to outlive us in any normal expectation of life events. Children always represent that sense of immortality, since a part of us should be passed on genetically to future generations of Basques. Yes, that too. I'm now an interloper.

However welcoming the people of Glasgow are to me—and I appreciate their efforts—I've lost my roots, with no chance of retrieving them. My sense of identity has been shattered. Without a language, expression is futile. Foreign translations can never convey my emotions. No home. No culture. It's like being in some form of suspended animation. I don't belong anywhere. I am a refugee. An immigrant here. Nostalgia and homesickness are intermingling. Why did I survive? Why couldn't it have been me that the Germans extinguished instead of you, my wife, and my children?

Is this the guilt of the survivor? I have so much anger and regret. All the things I should have done with you, my son and daughter, during your short lives. The hope and optimism were reduced to despair and cynicism. But what they can't take away from me are my memories of you. The good times we had together, playing pelota. Our summer holidays were spent on the beach at San Sebastian. Learning to swim. Learning how to ride a bike.

Just by visualising these events and experiences, I can bring you back to life in my imagination. Eskerrik asko. Thank you. One day, I know, I will be reunited with you all in Heaven. May God forgive me for killing one of Franco's men on my way here! Otherwise—but let's not go there—otherwise, I will be sent to hell.

That surely can't be any worse than the living hell I am enduring in my head every day. It's time to close now. I look forward to our reunion. Until then, to my emaztea, Naiara, my semea, Aitor, and my alaba, Agurtzane, I say, Maite zaitut (I love you) and Faltan zaitut (I will miss you). Agur (Farewell and goodbye).

Yours eternally,
Asier

Asier, Glasgow

Can I turn back time? Can I rewrite history? Can I undo all the evil captured so poignantly in Picasso's painting of my home town of Guernica? I am a doctor. Doctors are supposed to heal wounds. But first, I must heal myself. I know very well that physical wounds can, in many cases, be patched up. Perhaps there will always be something like a scar to remember them by. A disfigured face, maybe, or a limp? At least the world must acknowledge these marks as evidence of the suffering war has caused. But what about the psychological damage?

I feel I should now—after the trauma of Guernica—have acquired some superhuman powers: maybe even the ability to travel backwards and forwards through time. I say 'through' time, but understanding what I now know, it might be more accurate to speak about travelling *above* or *around* time. 'History repeats itself', so the old saying goes, and it seems that once again the world is poised, as if on a precipice.

As I start to pull myself back together again like a latter-day humpty-dumpty, I realise that I have no use for the king's army in this process. But back to my time-travel. Can I somehow reverse the suffering of war? Well, if that's not a realistic proposition, I know one that is. I can use my skills as a doctor to treat the casualties of war. But even better than that, I can also use them to treat the sick and infirm. In a way, isn't that a bit like turning back time: putting them back to their old self?

Steady! Why can't I keep my hand still? I used to be a skilled surgeon; whatever good can I do with the permanent DTs? Still, doctoring is not all about surgery, there's lots more *hands-off* than *hands-on* work. I'm sure I can be of some use to someone. But who's going to mend my broken heart? That'll never happen. So, what do I do? Just doing something, anything, to take my mind off the rumination. 'Stop!' I keep remembering to say to myself. Say it within two seconds and the negative idea can't take hold!

'Doctor, heal thyself!' Well, yes, I suppose I ought to know how to do this with all my training. But it's a different kettle of fish when you're working on your *own* mind and body. As a doctor, when you treat a patient, you know that people put their total trust in your judgement, and this gives you authority and confidence. Without confidence in his work, what good is a doctor? But as I was saying, treating my own mind and body is more of a challenge: there's no way I'm going to have total trust in this guy whose inadequacies and shortcomings I know only too well.

And as for respecting his authority, well, there's no real power differential any more, is there? He's my equal: how can I possibly agree to do as I am told?

So, what would a doctor normally do when faced with this conundrum? I suppose he'd talk to a friend. But I can't do this. I am alone. Any friends I may have had are either dead or thousands of miles away in Guernica. And I'd better not resort to imaginary friends, that way lies insanity. I suppose I can read my medical books, the few I managed to salvage in my hasty retreat from my homeland. One advantage I might have over my colleagues who haven't been there, is my personal experience of a patient's trauma in wartime. I think that does cast a whole new light on my predicament.

This song is by Katie Melua and appears on the compilation album *The Tracks That Got Away (2012)*.

Market Day in Guernica

My children played a skipping
game On market day in Guernica
On market day before they came
Before they came to Guernica.
I search my soul but cannot
start to find forgiveness in
my heart. My little ones no longer play
In Guernica on market day.

My father wore his linen suit
On market day in Guernica.
He always sold the finest fruit
Before they came to Guernica.

Now there's no way to let him
know How much I loved and miss
him so I watched as he was blown away

In Guernica on market day.
Away, Away
All blown
Away

My children played a skipping
game On market day in Guernica
On market day before they came
Before they came to Guernica.

I search my soul but cannot
start to find forgiveness in
my heart. My little ones no
longer play
In Guernica on market day.

That date will remain indelibly imprinted on my psyche. The day the Germans came to Guernica. Of course, it's taken me a while to take it in, but I do remember it was a Monday. Later, I worked out the actual date.

Zer ordu da? What time is it? Nothing makes any sense any more. *Emaztea* She's dead. What's the point of going on? Got to stop thinking like this. Lost everything. STOP! But it's true. Who am I? A man without a family. A man without a home *hasiera*. A man without a language. I might as well be invisible. I'm a foreigner. An outsider. They're nice enough folk, here, and I will be eternally grateful to the man who saved my life and brought me here.

I know I'll only stop these suicidal thoughts if I find something useful to do. I am a doctor, for Heaven's sake. There must be some small contribution I can make. Must stop dwelling on my own misery and start thinking of others. Certainly, there is a great need to help, here in Glasgow.

Have another look at my medical books. *Anatomia. Zirkulazio-aparatuko. Immunitate-sistema. Muskulu. NERBIOAK!* Well, yes, I've got plenty of nerves. And doubtless many others are suffering with their nerves. Ashlin seems very nice. I feel I can relate to her. She's a nurse. Perhaps we have something in common. I noticed how she gave me encouragement whenever I started talking about health matters. Maybe she can be the catalyst that can speed up my reactions and awaken me from this inertia.

Visited Bellahouston Park today. Officially opened by King George VI a couple of weeks ago. I like these parks. They do contrast so starkly with the poverty and misery I see all around me. Is it just the weather? No wonder the Brits go on about it all the time. I suppose we just take good weather for granted, back in Euskadi. Walking in nearby Victoria Park helps. It seems therapeutic. Like dreaming in many ways. Maybe I should try sleep-walking and combine the two?

5 War Diaries

By all accounts, Ashlin was the glue that held the trio together. She was small, graceful, strong, assertive, compassionate, elegant, determined and pretty, all rolled into one.

Through all the darkness that surrounded us, Ashlin was always our light.

John Oswald.

Ashlin's Diary

Growing up, my overriding emotion was fear. Fear of loss, fear of death. Fear of embarrassing the Oswald name. As landowners, we were looked upon as gentry and always had to set a good example. All I've ever wanted to do was escape. Torn in two, I appreciated all the Oswalds had done for John and me, but at the same time, I longed for a quiet life with our parents and the Ritchie name.

I think it was our parents' accident that spurred me on to become a nurse. Watching their lives being snatched away was dreadful. Watching their lives being snatched away with no one doing a thing was even worse.

Apart from the formalities of being an Oswald, pre-war life was quite good. John and I both graduated from Glasgow University with joint honours. John got a joint honours in Journalism and Spanish and I got a joint honours in Nursing and Business Studies.

When John returned to Scotstoun with Asier, they were both in a bad way. At that time, I was working at Glasgow Western Infirmary as well as helping to set up Killearn Hospital.

Killearn Hospital was one of five commissioned in 1938 in preparation for the war. Building started in 1939 and was complete in 1941 in time for the air raids on Clydebank and other Clydeside towns, which could be seen and heard in Killearn

After Guernica, John went straight back to work. This was John's way of dealing with things: he'd just bury his feelings and focus on something else. This worried me. Asier, on the other hand, was slowly working through his pain.

In 1940, he felt ready to work again. We decided to open a business together: a doctor's surgery servicing the shipyards. We also used the surgery for social purposes. Asier insisted on setting up what the Spanish call a *tertulia*, a social gathering with literary, political, or artistic overtones. The aim of this was to keep spirits high, especially during winter. The thought of war scared me. I couldn't bear to lose John. At this point, all I could do was hope for the best and prepare for the worst.

Ashlin's Diary 1937-1945
1937

That's men for you! Always have to be off somewhere seeking adventure. Interfering in the affairs of other countries that really don't concern them. Charity begins at home. Plenty of useful things John could have been doing here in Scotland. Fighting for workers' rights, for a start. But no, that would be just far too provincial for John. His aims are far more international, so he claims. I just don't get it. How can you 'care' for someone thousands of miles away?

For me, caring is something you do out of love. Consequently, it's perfectly understandable that we care for those closest to us, our loved ones. Beyond that, I feel, we have a duty to care for the vulnerable souls in the community, and that's why I chose to become a nurse in the first place. But surely that *Weltschmerz*, as the Germans call it, can't really be about caring? How can you empathise with someone you've never met who lives on the other side of the world? It's true they are human beings, just like us, but surely, it's the job of people in their own community to look after them.

John's a journalist. An investigative journalist. That might explain his curiosity about what's happening in Spain, but I worry. I worry that curiosity killed the cat. These young men seem to have been radicalised by someone or something. Is it just boredom that leads them to want to go and fight? I think it's the excitement that appeals to them. I suppose I should be grateful for small mercies: at least John hasn't joined Oswald Mosley's black shirts. I don't understand politics. There's talk of Lord Halifax doing a deal with Hitler to avoid war.

'Follow the money', everybody tells me: it's all about the industrialists clinching economic deals. Strange bedfellows, Hitler and Chamberlain, probably a marriage of convenience against the perceived common enemy: Communism and its threat to the British monarchy. "No difference between the British and the Germans," says Hitler. "We are all ultimately both a part of the Aryan race."

Now this young doctor John has brought back to Glasgow is a bit of a conundrum. John was quick to correct me when I called him a Spaniard. "Asier is a proud Basque!" His command of the English language is pretty good for a foreigner, but he seems to have some difficulty understanding people from round here. I have to admit, I quite like Asier. Maybe it's because we are both interested in medicine. We could certainly make good use of a person with his skills as a doctor in Glasgow.

1938

The Shipbuilders on Clydebank are justifiably proud of their work. And today we witnessed the culmination of that work with the launch of HMS Queen Elizabeth. Not that the lads are ever likely to be sailing on her themselves. She's a luxury ship, built for folk with lots of money. But the gentleman from John

Brown's Shipyards has been an absolute angel. He's helped Asier and me to establish a surgery quite close by. Of course, there is a degree of enlightened self-interest on his part. His workers are always losing fingers in the machinery.

It's a really dangerous job but we patch the men up as best we can, and very soon it's back to work for them. The payments we get from their employers for treatment help to pay for those in the community with no money to cover medical expenses.

John's really depressed. After barely a year, the International Brigades have returned from Spain, and Franco's side is clearly winning, if there ever can be winners in a civil war.

We are very busy, Asier and I, at the surgery, every day. We hardly ever get a chance to discuss the causes of all this sickness in the community. But when we do, our conclusions are quite startling. After only a moment's reflection, Asier sees the root of the problem, whereas it takes much longer for me. It's that insider/outsider thing. Because I've grown up with all the poverty and pollution, I just take it all for granted, whereas Asier gets a much more objective view of Glasgow. Access to a plentiful supply of clean water would make a big difference.

1939

The more I think about it, the more I realise that there is a serious gulf between how men see the world and how women see it. Of course, growing up alongside my brother gave me some insight into how men think, but working with Asier has demonstrated this fact on another level entirely. Asier has the clinical mind of a medic. He seems to be almost cold and calculating at all times. I suppose he would have needed that temperament in the days when he was able to perform surgery. He hasn't had a steady hand since Guernica.

He always wants to 'fix' the patients, whilst I can often see that their priority is having someone to listen. In a way, I suppose, the roles of nurse and doctor complement each other very well. Like a well-functioning marriage, perhaps? I honestly can't tell how Asier feels about me. He never shows his emotions. He definitely doesn't wear his heart on his sleeve. As for me, I find him rather attractive, but I daren't declare an interest just yet, because I'd be mortified if he didn't reciprocate my affections. Oh, and yes, it's 1939, Britain and Germany are now officially at war.

1940

After working so hard during the week, it's really nice to relax at the weekend. Of course, it's good that, like myself, Asier is a regular church-goer, and the pair of us visit the local Catholic church at least once a week (even though I'm not Catholic). I hadn't realised until Asier informed me of the fact that the Jesuits are so closely tied up with the Basques. Belonging. That's what life is all about. Tribalism, John calls it. For me, it's my family, my community and my religion. For John, it seems to be more about football, and which team you support.

I'd like to think that it's about what we have in common rather than what divides us. Divide and conquer: isn't that what the Establishment believes? Set the plebs against each other, and they'll never notice that you're their class enemy. However, once war has been declared, different rules apply. We're all on the same side now. Against an external enemy. The Nazis, or the Communists, take your pick.

1941

On the nights of 13 and 14 March 1941, the nearby town of Clydebank was largely destroyed and suffered the worst destruction and civilian loss of life in all of Scotland. 528 people died, 617 people were seriously injured, and hundreds more were injured by blast debris. Out of approximately 12,000 houses, only 7 remained undamaged.

As the bombs got closer and louder, Asier and I huddled up in our garden shelter. I was terrified. At that point, I remembered what my mother would say to me: "If you are ever really frightened, close your eyes and add a little courage. Soon your feelings will turn to excitement."

I began to think. Maybe I'm looking at all this war business wrong. As awful as things were, the whole neighbourhood and country were working closer than ever. We may be underdogs but we held the moral high ground. Exciting or frightening?

When I opened my eyes, I said, without thinking, "Asier, make love to me."

"*Que?*" he replied.

"We could be dead any minute. I want to make the most of every moment," I said.

"*Si,*" he replied. Afterwards, I thanked him. He was so laidback. "*De nada,*" was his casual reply. On surviving the Blitz, we became much closer and this

31

became a private joke before making love: 'I think I hear the drone of planes', one of us would say.

The flames of the carnage could be seen as far out as Shotts in Lanarkshire. The war had come to our doorstep and was suddenly very real indeed. Stories of heartbreak, honour and despair roll in every day now.

I suppose, in hindsight, Clydesdale Docks was an obvious target for the Germans. But to return with a follow-up attack during the aftermath was clearly a planned move. Whether the idea was to intimidate the Scots in the hopes that we would beg the UK government to sue for peace is still unclear. In any event, it didn't work: it strengthened our resolve against the Nazis.

Who, incidentally, is about to attack the Russians, so John informs me. "What an awful time to bring a baby into the world," protests the midwife. "And yet, with such carnage on the battlefield, I suppose we'll be needing population regeneration, looking at the situation dispassionately, as the Establishment do." I realise how important our job is going to be in ensuring that pregnancies are brought to healthy resolutions through the expectant mothers getting sound advice.

Asier and I wish our job generally were more about avoiding the need for intervention at a late stage in an ailment's progression, but quite honestly, all we can do in most cases is administer first aid, In wartime, it's more like fire-fighting.

Asier and I felt that it was not only our job to protect the health of the shipyard workers and people, but to help raise their spirits too. Asier had come through the bombing of Guernica and was even more determined than ever. All we can do is keep busy.

As luck would have it, all three of us both like and can play music. The boys have guitars—Asier is particularly good at flamenco style—and I am eternally grateful that my family always encouraged me to go to piano lessons. We've even got a regular spot at the local pub now!

1942

January again! And freezing temperatures into the bargain. But I've found a way to stay warm at night. And I don't mean a hot water bottle!

Asier's been busy shovelling away the snow. We have to get to our place of work. Our patients have grown to rely on us. He's been asking me what the Steamie's all about. "Women's issues!" I reply, and assume he'll find it too embarrassing to press me further on the matter. But he persists, so I explain that, whilst fulfilling a necessary function— i.e., laundry—the Steamie is like the local gossip shop, and it allows the women to let off steam! He understands its social as well as its psychological purpose.

Rationing's causing problems on several fronts simultaneously: both soap and milk are in short supply, and both of these have an impact on our patients' health. Some good news in the pipeline, though: the National Health Service is going to be free, and that includes free milk, as well as all the essential vitamins. We're surely going to be needing more staff with the inevitable surge in demand, now that services are going to be free.

The back courts are used for all sorts. When we start work, we see women hanging out their washing. The wind freshens up old clothes and leaves them smelling fresh and clean (A walk in Victoria Park does the same thing for my head). We are often working late and I sometimes watch the women leaning out of their windows watching their kids, or some singers who drop by. It's a real amphitheatre of activity!

1943

A free health service is a good start but until we tackle poverty, lack of adequate housing with adequate heating, poor sanitation and above all, limited education, we are fighting a losing battle. Yes, it's fantastic that we now have antibiotics to fight the illnesses that used to be a death sentence to the already infirm, as well as the very young or the old. Life expectancy for most people here in parts of Glasgow is barely retirement age. Maybe one day, in the not-too-distant future, people will survive well into their seventies!

1944

I was thinking what an amazing feat Asier has achieved in mastering the English language. And not just that. He is actually beginning to understand the Glaswegian accent, too. We sing and play music together because music's a universal language, but comedy's a different kettle of fish entirely. I try to tell him that it's the very spontaneity that makes a joke a joke, so if I have to explain a joke to him, not only do I potentially miss the next joke through his interruption, but it won't even be funny for him.

To pay me back, Asier offered to take me to see a film in Spanish. I should add that it didn't even have subtitles. I suppose it was quite a gamble putting on such a film in Glasgow at the time, but at least it allowed the cultured *cognoscenti* to pretend they understood.

Another film in Spanish, but this time it's one of Disney's cartoons, *los tres caballeros*, so not too challenging for me this time. They reckon we'll soon be getting television back again. Another Scottish invention. They had to stop broadcasting during the war years. Hoping we'll soon be able to buy a decent radio. The reception on the one at home is so hit-and-miss.

1945

And we're off to the pictures again. The Pathé newsreels are always very informative. And then there's those none-too-subtle Government Information Films. The one today was all about healthy eating, because now we have a socialist government in the UK. Asier's a nervous wreck today. I forgot to tell him that we let off fireworks on 5 November. Evidently, the explosions triggered bad memories of wartime experiences for him. He's got me a Christmas present. Something that was hard to come by during the war.

I try to feign gratitude for his gift, but fear he doesn't know the difference between perfume and scent! I often think it would be much simpler if men just handed us cash and let us select our chosen fragrances or underwear, but I suppose it's really the thought that counts.

James

Dr Asier Santamaria's diary comes in the form of a time-line. It is clear and concise. He seems to have used some of the Basque language. (We have tried our best not to confuse, using dates, where possible, throughout the book as we jump back and forth through time.)

Selena and I spoke at length about Asier's diary. "As a foreign national in a different country, it can be really frustrating communicating, especially when you don't have the words to say what you really want to say," said Selena. We have done our best to translate Asier's diaries and have come up with the following:

Asier's War Diary
Igandea, 1937 Uztaila 29

We spoke Spanish back home too. We had to. So, we grew up bilingual. That made it quite easy to pick up other languages. France was, in one way, just an extension of our *Pays Basques*, so naturally we learned to communicate with our near neighbours. And Portuguese came quite easily, too, just over the border in the opposite direction. In school, we learned English, because we saw the business advantages.

But what were these Glaswegians speaking? It didn't sound much like the English we had to recite. And even once I'd realised that this was a very strong accent and therefore possibly decipherable, there was a whole new set of vocabulary to learn. At first, I thought everyone must be speaking Gaelic!

Everything made much more sense after a couple of drinks down the pub with the locals. Somehow that sense of community transcended any linguistic barrier. As an outsider, I was classless. And this helped when it came to treating my patients: there was no 'us and them'. For me, my patients were very much my equals.

Igandea, 1937 Urria 24

Picasso's *Guernica* has been on display in Paris for a few months now. I like the artist's ability to respond. Observing Guernica, that Gestapo guy asked him if he did this. To which Picasso characteristically replied, "No, *you* did!" Amazing feat. Considering the attack had only been one month before. We need them, our artists.

They help us understand the world around us. It helps bring history to life.

Igandea, 1937 Azaroa 28

Sometimes I find myself falling into a deep depression. I'm convinced the weather doesn't help. How do folk keep warm in this climate? Coal seems the only answer but it's expensive and not very good quality. You only have to examine the yellowing distemper and wallpaper to realise how much sulphur it contains. Can't be very healthy. *Lambrotsuan.* The fog mixes with the smoke. They call it SMOG here. Sometimes you can't even see where you're going. And the SMOG is yellow, too, if not brown. They cough it up all the time, especially the malnourished kids and older folk. Life expectancy is poor here. They're middle-aged (statistically speaking) by the time they're thirty!

Igandea, 1937 Abendua 26

It's Christmas. I suppose that does raise your spirits. Christmas makes me think of family and times gone by.

Osteguna, 1938 Urtarrila 6

We always celebrated epiphany. Will this be my epiphany? The year when the whole point of this mental suffering is revealed to me? It's just that right now I see it more in the apocalyptical images of Picasso's mural. Shining a light on Franco's dirty little secret. Whatever I may think of the artist and his morals, I feel sure that his painting will endure much longer than any statue of Franco.

Osteguna, 1938 Otsaila 4

The release of Disney's *Snow White and the Seven Dwarfs*, a particular favourite of Josef Goebbels, coincides with Hitler's takeover of the German army, putting fellow Nazis into key posts. It's getting worrying, now. Once a dictator commands the military, everyone else is powerless to influence his decisions.

Astelehena, 1938 Martxoa 28

As Easter approaches, I ask the children that I treat what it means for them. Usually, it's rolling boiled eggs, though, occasionally, one of them will pick up on its Christian significance. I tell them all about the *pasos* back home. I remember clearly how our children enjoyed staying up late to view the torchlight processions with many ancient relics being carried through the town.

Larunbata, 1938 Maiatza 14

Now to more practical matters. Ashlin and I have set up a surgery near the shipyards. A director from John Brown's Shipyards helped us get the business off the ground. I think we'll be able to subsidise our poorer patients through guaranteed fees from the shipyards. We met Number 9 Company of the Glasgow ARP (Air Raid Precaution squads) to help them treat casualties with first aid in the event of war.

Living next door to the surgery was Big Josie. She was, originally from Ireland, 6 feet 4 inches tall and weighed around 17 stone. She worked as a labourer in Tod & MacGregor shipyards, and latterly as a farm worker near Anniesland. Big Josie was sworn in as a special constable during the Partick Riots. Ashlin convinced her to work for us as a cleaner, receptionist, and guard. No one dared mess with her. Not even me!

Asteazkena, 1938 Maiatza 25

313 dead. I feel sympathy for my fellow human beings. One day, it's Guernica, the next it's Alicante. To me, there's nothing chivalrous about modern warfare. It seems such a cowardly act to attack from the air when you've practically little or no resistance from below. Civil War, they call it. I beg to differ. Nothing civil about it.

Astelehena, 1938 Ekaina 6

Sigmund Freud has arrived in England. I'm sure there will be plenty of shell-shock cases for him to unravel. I never was convinced of the need for "mad doctors" until now. We can heal their wounds, but how can we heal their souls? That's more like a job for a priest, I would think.

Big Josie has got everyone calling me Santa. Apparently, my name was too hard for people to remember. In the Basque Country, we have our own Santa. In the Basque Country, the equivalent of Santa is Olentzero, and he lives or lived (depending on what you believe) in the mountains, and he wears the boy's *casera*. He is a mythical Basque character who is widely portrayed as a messenger who cries out that it is Christmas time throughout all the corners of the Basque Country. In some versions, the Olentzero is a farmer or a shepherd. Nevertheless, it is common in all of the tales that the Olentzero brings good news to people.

He is also known as the coal man who comes down from the mountains on his *pottok* (wild Basque horse) to hand out presents to children. Chestnuts and wine are given to the villagers. By tradition, on 24 December, the Basque radio stations broadcast that Olentzero had begun his journey from the mountains to children's homes.

Olentzero was banned as a symbol of regional separatism.

I think I deserve a little distraction now. I do like jazz. Benny Goodman, Fats Waller and Ella Fitzgerald. I could listen to that music all night. But I must search long and hard to find a station that plays my kind of music. There's Arty Shaw playing *Begin the Beguine*. And what's this? Sounds like German and yet it's on the BBC. Oh, now I hear it more clearly: it's the Andrews Sisters singing *Bei mir bist du schön*.

Asteartea, 1938 Iraila 27

It's been a wonderful day today. Now, I'm no avid monarchist, but I must admit that the Brits do these things in some style. We all went down to Clydebank to witness the launching of a big ship. It (or should I say 'she') was named Queen Elizabeth, after King George VI's wife. Of course, they couldn't have named her Queen Elizabeth I, for historically obvious reasons! What a waste of champagne, though!

Ostirala, 1938 Iraila 30

Chamberlain? What's he up to? Does he really regard Adolf Hitler as a man of integrity? Well, I see he's been to meet the man in Berchtesgarden. And now, he's off to Munich to get the Führer's autograph. Not worth the paper it's written on, though it may have considerable value as a collector's piece, years into the future.

Igandea, 1938 Urria 30

I know I go on about how bad the reception is on this antiquated radio, but it provides a life-line. There's nothing more frustrating than being kept in the dark. At least I can move the dial to pick up a different station if I don't believe what I'm hearing on the BBC. Propaganda, mostly. And so out of date by the time it's all been sanitised by the mandarins. Hitler realises the power of the media and he has ensured that every German citizen has a wireless set. With a minister actually in charge of propaganda, namely Goebbels, he knows how to control the people. It is almost thought control.

Asteazkena, 1938 Azaroa 9

Kristallnacht, they call it. Lots of broken glass. Who are the scapegoats? The Jews, of course. The Nazis have been working up towards this day. It starts with being ostracised. Then demonisation. Then they use the cinemas to make associations in the mind between rats and Jews. Leni Riefenstahl was brilliant at film-making. But as far as Spanish film-makers are concerned, I never could understand where Luis Bunuel's allegiances lay. Which side was he on?

Asteartea, 1938 Azaroa 15

The International Brigades are going home. At least they tried. My friend was proud to be a member. Does this mean the Spanish Civil War is over, perhaps? Not a chance! Franco and his cohorts are in the ascendency.

Larunbata, 1938 Abendua 31

Time to reflect. After more than a year spent in Glasgow, what have I achieved? I don't want to blow my own trumpet. It's not what people hereabouts do. But in retrospect, I think I can justifiably highlight some of my medical successes. Such a lot of avoidable illnesses, I think. Many are directly attributable to poor sanitation. I was quite surprised to find instances of cholera, for example. I came across smallpox, diphtheria, scarlet fever and typhus. And measles mumps and whooping cough were a regular occurrence. What else could have been prevented?

Well, there was that ghastly pollution caused no doubt by heavy industry and the burning of coal. That accounts for the respiratory diseases. And consumption or TB as it is known here. If the pollution wasn't bad enough, the heavy smoking made it worse, but then, who could begrudge them their fags? A necessary evil for calming the nerves, and there were plenty of folk suffering from their nerves. And last of all was the big 'C'. The illness must not, under any circumstances, be named.

For me, the hardest thing was to see children suffering. I did my best, and Ashlin really helped me with their treatment. But it's so frustrating to bring them in for treatment, knowing they will be returning to the very slum-like conditions that caused the illness in the first place: poor nutrition, lack of adequate heating, dampness.

Osteguna, 1939 Urtarrila 26

Franco has regained Barcelona. Doesn't help our opposition when countries like Belgium reinstate trade with Franco.

Asteartea, 1939 Otsaila 28

So that's it. First Holland, and now France and Great Britain recognise Franco's government. But the *Anderson Shelters* are going up, so they must be expecting war with Germany.

Larunbata, 1939 Apirila 1

No, it's no April fool's joke. Franco's back in Madrid. And Americas recognised him as the legitimate government of Spain. Even Pope Pius XII has congratulated him!

Asteartea, 1939 Maiatza 30

Do I question my faith? Of course, I do. My faith is constantly tested. How can God allow such atrocities to happen? Sometimes, when I fear that death is imminent—perhaps from a German bombing raid—I cling on to my Catholic beliefs tenaciously. I find solace in our local church. And yet, when my eyes get clouded by the rational scientist within me, pure scepticism is the result.

Ostirala,1939 Ekaina 30

Then there's politics. I'm drawn towards those with more socialist credentials here in Scotland. I think it's because they're hoping for reforms in the health service. I think it's disgraceful that the poverty-stricken underclass is expected to pay for the services of a doctor. I just can't bear the idea of taking money from someone so much worse-off than me.

Igandea, 1939 Uztaila 30

Ashlin's nice, and she's also a very caring human being. Health is so much more than diagnosis and treatment by a male doctor. Most of the recovery comes from the nurturing qualities that a female can bring to the process. She's such a loving person, much like my wife was.

Astazkena, 1939 Abuztua 23

After Stalin requested an anti-Nazi pact, he and Churchill both signed it, but it shows how little we can trust him when just four months later, he signed a pact with the Nazis, and they're carving up Eastern Europe between them.

Osteguna, 1939 Abuztua 31

They're evacuating the kids here in Clydebank. It's going to be very strange without them around. They're probably being sent to rural locations, but imagine the uncertainty: arriving with a new 'family'. Would you be trusting of adults or suspicious? I dare say, for some kids, it might have been some big adventure, a chance to get away from the Big Smoke, too. Perhaps their health will improve.

Ostirala, 1939 Irailia 1

Hitler's decided to exterminate the mentally ill (not including himself, of course!). I wish those Nazi doctors would recognise the illogicality of their position on eugenics. Any fool knows that inbreeding can have horrendous consequences. Pedigree animals may look good but their offspring often show genetic faults. Exogenesis is how we help edit out mistakes. As a Basque, I've looked carefully at this concept, because I realise that we have kept our race pure through *not* interbreeding. Indeed, unlike over here, it is quite common for cousins to marry in Euskadi. Whether that leads to mental illnesses is debatable.

Igandea, 1939 Irailia 3

Lebensraum, the Germans call it. They never seem content with their own little plot of land. They always have to encroach on other people's territory. Just look at the speed at which their empire is growing northwards to the far-flung polar regions; southwards and into Africa; eastwards into Poland and out towards Russia; and now—so it would appear—even the United Kingdom is in their sights.

I had, perhaps naively, thought that I would at last be safe in Scotland after my miraculous escape from Guernica, and yet, barely two years on, I am seriously contemplating a scenario where the German Luftwaffe may attack me once again, but this time in Glasgow. 'Out of the frying-pan into the fire', as the Brits say! Perhaps I'd be better off returning to Euskadi?

But wait a minute! Of course, I can't possibly go back there. Franco has my name on his hit-list. However much I regret killing that poor man, regardless of the fact that he was fighting for the Fascist cause, contrition would not be a mitigating factor. I would be unceremoniously eliminated, were I to return to Spain.

No, my destiny is here, in Glasgow, where I can put my medical skills to good use. Nice of the Glaswegians not to lock me up with all the other undesirable aliens. I've heard that Whitehall has determined that anyone with a German-sounding name shall be detained for the duration of the war. Ironically, of course, this will include many Jews. And, as for Spaniards (which the Brits probably wouldn't be able to differentiate from us Basques), well, they would similarly be deemed to be a threat under a leader like Franco, and given the British mistrust of all Latin types, I could well be taken for an Italian, and duly incarcerated along with all the other presumed Nazi sympathisers.

Osteguna, 1939 Iraila 14

He's here! Churchill in Scotland! (Well, Scapa Flow, to be precise.) Something's coming. I'm sure of it.

Astertea, 1939 Iraila 19

There's Lord Haw-Haw on the wireless, from *Reichsrundfunk*, Berlin. Is he Irish, British or American? Maybe whichever is most expedient at the time.

Larunbata, 1939 Urria 14

Churchill must be psychic. A U-boat's torpedoed the Royal Oak in Scapa Flow, Orkney. The saddest thing about it is the number of young men who died: 120 young sailors between the ages of fourteen and eighteen.

Astelehena, 1939 Urria 16

Heinkel bombers have hit a base near Edinburgh. No alarm went off. Everyone seems to have been taken off guard. Our side did shoot down a couple of planes, though, and took some of the first German prisoners-of-war, it would appear. The Spitfires seem to have triumphed on this occasion.

Larunbata, 1939 Urria 28

A Heinkel-111 has been shot down by a spitfire. Right here in Scotland.

Astelehena, 1939 Abendua 25

The kids are back! Those evacuees from way back in August. Seems like the Germans aren't willing to sacrifice their bombs in a Blitzkrieg over Glasgow, though we had seriously expected them to do so.

Astelehena, 1940 Urtarrila 8

Well, maybe some good will come of all this rationing. Today, I hear, they've started to ration butter, sugar and bacon. The health of the nation, ironically, will benefit from this. And not just people's teeth (which are, by the way, in a parlous state!).

Asteazkena, 1940 Otsaila 28

The Ministry of Food says we must dig for victory. By which they mean turning all our parks and gardens into vegetable plots. We are an island. This has advantages and disadvantages. It makes us harder to invade, perhaps, but also makes us vulnerable because we import so much of our food from abroad.

Igandea, 1940 Martzoa 31

So many preventable illnesses here. If we could only persuade the mothers to get their children vaccinated against these common, but often deadly diseases.

Asteartea, 1940 Apirila 30

I took one of my constitutional walks today. Walking is so good for the soul. And the wind! I love a cool breeze. It blows your cares away. Loch Lomond reminds me of the wetlands back in Euskadi. Hard to believe that Glasgow is so close to such a beautiful, wild terrain.

Osteguna, 1940 Maiatza 30

Neville Chamberlain had been a pacifier. This was never going to be an acceptable response to a character like Hitler. Any psychiatrist could see that the man exhibited delusions of grandeur. The British have a saying: 'Set a thief to catch a thief'. In wartime, Britain needed a leader whose very sanity during peacetime would be in question. Like Hitler, Churchill displayed many characteristics of the psychopath. Crucially, he was never troubled by any of the scruples that a more empathic individual might have had about the loss of life. The latter was, for him, simply a necessary ingredient during wartime.

Igandea, 1940 Ekaina 9

Next in line for invasion were the Benelux countries along with Northern France. I now see why Hitler was only too happy to assist Franco by bombing Guernica. For the Nazis, along with other Spanish towns, it provided an experimental theatre of war where cutting-edge weaponry could be tested out. The lightning strikes that the Luftwaffe delivered now in the countries of Western Europe were defined by the German term, *Britzkrieg*. Whilst, as part of their own propaganda drive, the British were outlawing German vocabulary—

Diesel, for example, was renamed DERV—the *Blitz* was to be a *Fremdwort* indelibly written onto their language.

Astelehena, 1940 Ekaina 10

So now the battle lines are drawn: Japan, Germany and Italy are set against Britain, Russia and France, with no sign of the Americans, yet. Neutrality is good for business, so it seems. Switzerland holds a similar view.

Ostirala, 1940 Ekaina 14

What's Franco up to now? The Spanish have invaded Tangier in Morocco. Has he got ambitions to take Gibraltar off the British?

And now he's sending Spanish workers off to Germany to help keep their industry going. With so many Germans in the military, I suppose Hitler needs these *Fremdarbeiter.*

Igandea, 1940 Ekaina 30

They've taken the Channel Islands. Where will the Nazis strike next?

Asteazkena, 1940 Uztaila 10

Zer ordu da? What time is it? What day is today? Wednesday? Is this a nightmare, or do I seem to be experiencing some kind of *déjà vu*? The Germans are here in the skies above the United Kingdom just like they were only three years ago in Euskadi. Or am I just having flashbacks to Guernica?

Blitzkrieg, they call it. Something's different here. The Brits are fighting back! Not so easy when you meet some resistance, is it, Fritz? We're getting a very unclear picture of what's going on. Churchill's put a blackout on reporting, in case it helps the enemy. Even so, from the limited information available, London's getting it hard.

I'm sure we'll be next. They always go after major industrial areas, and Glasgow's one of them. They'll be trying to incapacitate the shipbuilding. It's relentless. Can't sleep. Dare not sleep. Those sirens! Like Pavlov's dog I am. Whenever I hear the air raid warning, I panic. It must be the same for everyone. And the Anderson Shelters aren't much use either. "Turn that light out," the warden says to me. "Don't you know there's a war on?" Bloody hard to read in the dark, though.

Anderson Shelters

In March 1940, a central control centre was set up in Clydebank Library so that, in the event of an air attack on Clydebank, emergency operations such as fire-fighting and first aid could be coordinated properly. Although most people did not think that Clydebank would be bombed, many families had air raid shelters by this time, which they shared with their neighbours. Most of these were Anderson Shelters which came as a kit of 6 sheets of steel which were bolted together and partly dug into the ground.

Some facts about Anderson Shelters: When built they were 6 feet high, 4 feet wide and 6½ feet long. They were made to stand in a pit 4 feet deep (which is why they often flooded) and also had 15 inches of earth heaped on the roof. The council delivered the shelters but the home owner had to put them up. Shelters were free if you earned below £250 a year. Otherwise, they were £6 14s or £10 18s. Some people fitted bunk beds, others slept on deck chairs. The shelters were named after Sir John Anderson, who was home secretary in 1933 when they were being issued. The shelter offered protection against anything except a direct hit.

Asteakzena, 1940 Iraila 11

Apart from the devastation in London and the South East, generally, there has been considerable damage inflicted on the House of Hannover at Buckingham Palace. Is nothing sacred? The Royals are Germans, for goodness sake!

Igandea, 1940 Iraila 22

Strange bedfellows indeed. We've always realised that Spain, Italy and Germany would make common causes under the banner of Fascism. But Japan? Seriously? Journalist George Steer could see the parallels between his experiences as a reporter in Ethiopia with those in my beloved Basque Country. What do Franco, Mussolini, Hitler and Hirohito have in common? *Mis*-leaders to a man.

Asteazkena, 1940 Urria 30

I've never seen women take so naturally to what has always been regarded as 'men's work'; and I don't just mean keeping the farms going to supply the nation with food. Some braver souls had jobs in the munitions factories cooking up the 'devil's porridge'.

Larunbata, 1940 Azaroa 23

I took Ashlin to the Cosmo, an arthouse cinema in Rose Street in the centre of Glasgow, not far from Sauchiehall Street. Rather appropriately, the film we saw was *The Great Dictator* starring Charlie Chaplin. Ironically, too, Chaplin and Hitler shared the same date of birth. After the film, we strolled down Sauchiehall Street. I was impressed by the height of the Beresford Hotel. Such skyscrapers were more often to be seen in America.

Igandea, 1940 Abendua 22

Made my weekly visit to church this morning. Nothing unusual there, but I just love hearing Mass in Latin. I know it's sometimes thought too exclusive, keeping the Word of God within the clergy, and setting up unnecessary obstacles to the laity. But, for me, it's like having a common language all Catholics can share, regardless of where in the world they live. As Christmas approaches, I imagine a rebirth of our nation personified in the birth of Jesus Christ.

Asteartea, 1941 Urtarrila 21

The government don't like socialism. They've just banned the *Daily Worker,* as they see it as a propaganda tool of the Soviets. No similar condemnation of the *Daily Mail*, a tabloid supporting Oswald Mosley's black shirts, as far as I can see.

Asteartea, 1941 Otsaila 18

I went up to see George Square today. Both wealth and poverty are apparent in this town. Much of the wealth—let it not be forgotten—came from tobacco and slavery. There are constant reminders of this when you look around you in George Square. The other big industry is shipbuilding on the Clyde. Men who work there take an immense pride in their work.

Asteartea, 1941 Martxoa 14

I am literally speechless after what's just happened in Clydebank. I've copied this news report from the Glasgow Herald:

The cool, unwavering courage of the people is evident, and when the full story of their heroism in the face of the Luftwaffe is told, they will take their place alongside the citizens of London and Coventry.

Glasgow Herald, 18 March 1941

Bad enough to be bombed the first night, but to send another 200 bombers just when we're trying to salvage what we can—as well as hopefully save a few lives—well, that's unforgivable. John Brown's Shipyard was clearly their target. The Poles were right by our side shooting back at the Luftwaffe. This truly was the Clydebank's *Blitz.* But if this was supposed to frighten *Bankies* into a state of mind where they would beg the British government to sue for peace with Germany, it was a huge miscalculation, far from it. It only strengthened Clydebank, Glasgow, and Scotland's resolve to stand up to Hitler.

Osteguna, 1941 Apirila 3

I don't get it. Stalin lets Churchill down by forming a non-aggression pact with the Nazis and yet, Churchill is still quite happy to tip him off about the imminent invasion of Russia.

Larunbata, 1941 Maiatza 10

What was Hess thinking of, coming to Scotland? They say—but then who can believe such rumours—that he was bringing over a deal, coming directly on Hitler's instructions. We'll most probably never know the truth. Too sensitive. Even years into the future its contents could destabilise international relations.

Igandea, 1941 Ekaina 22

Is the man mad? What strategist could ever contemplate fighting on so many fronts simultaneously? So, Hitler's got 4 million pairs of boots on the ground bound for Russia. I have the distinct feeling that this is where he may meet his very own Waterloo.

Osteguna, 1941 Uztaila 10

Ashlin's been offering pre-natal classes to expectant mothers here. Education is so important if we're to keep them and their babies healthy. Some of them claim they don't even know how they got pregnant! And that's after they've already had 7 kids!

Asteazkena, 1941 Abuzua 20

I suppose the men working in shipbuilding are lucky in one way. At least, if they get sick, their employer has a vested interest in getting them patched up and back to work. This involves paying the doctor. Other men are less fortunate. I do what I can without expecting any recompense but there is a limit to the *pro bono* work a doctor can afford to do.

Larunbata, 1941 Urria 11

Took a tram out to Ibrox today. Brilliant game! Rangers won 7:0 against Hamilton. This is the kind of team I want to support. It gives me a feel-good sensation and motivation to dedicate myself to my medical emergencies. I suppose you could say that all Ashlin and I do is first aid. I've no problem with that. At least we're appreciated.

Larunbata, 1941 Azaroa 15

Ashlin and I decided to form a band. Nothing too serious. More for our own enjoyment really. There's me on guitar and Ashlin on piano. I suppose you could call what we play folk music. I like the fact that music is a universal language. I can sing the words of the *Tree of Guernica* in Basque and Ashlin can play along to accompany me. Eventually, I expect she will learn the words, too. After all, we managed to sing a Scottish song completely in Gaelic without fully understanding what we were singing about at a local pub. Nobody knew we were winging it!

Igandea, 1941 Abendua 7

There's talk of the Yanks getting involved in the war, finally. I can't believe they've been content to remain neutral for so long. Probably in their interests, though. Not sure what to believe any more. I also found out just about everyone has a nickname and that this extends to the armed forces:

"Our fighting men are makers of slang because they are adventurous individuals and they are not restricted by decorum and their taste is unlimited. Their hunting ground for new terms is in their native tongue as well as foreign. They adopt traditional devices of similitude, making attributes work for the whole. They use hidden resemblances, they know no limitations and have no boundaries. They have substituted far-fetched figures for a hundred literary descriptions, using abbreviations most freely, compositions, formations of words to resemble the sound and picturesque synonyms.

"Their transfer of proper names into common usage has been so much 'duck-soup' (that which is done with ease). They have enriched the national vocabulary with many new verbs and verb phrases. It must not be forgotten that our fighting men have come from all walks of life, that all sections and divisions of a free social order are represented and each man has brought the peculiar and Glasgow language of his section of the country with him. Ours is a fighting force of a hundred races and as many creeds speaking a language called American."

Words of the Fighting Forces, by Clinton A. Sanders and Joseph W. Blackwell, Jr., 1942.

Larunbata, 1942 Urtarrila 31

So, bloody cold! I don't usually swear but this month has been absolutely freezing. Add to that all that digging we've had to do to remove the snow. I have had to discourage the older folk from clearing their pathways of nearly 30 centimetres of snow because they could very easily die of a heart attack, not being used to such physical effort.

Larunbata, 1942 Otsaila 28

Now it's *soap* rationing, for goodness sake! It's hard enough to persuade the patients to wash as it is. And cleanliness is next to Godliness, as they say. Some of these old fellows will never take a bath. Hardly surprising in these freezing conditions, though. I've heard the zinc baths are used to bathe an entire family in front of the fire in the living room. There are some public baths, of course. And I'm wondering what the Steamies are all about?

Economist William Beveridge sets out his vision of a post-war Welfare State to banish from Britain the evils of the Five Giants—want, ignorance, squalor, idleness and disease.

1942 Beveridge Report published (I don't think Beveridge would have approved of benefits given his views about *idleness*!)

Osteguna, 1942 Apirila 30

I love the spring. Seeing the buds on the trees explode to reveal a prolific array of leaves. Different species of trees here, of course. But I recognise *pinus sylvestris*. Here they call it Scots Pine. We had the *quercus pyrenaica*, but *quercus robur* is the local variety of oak, though there are not many of them here in Scotland. I miss our *Juniperus thurifera*, but apart from that, I've seen many trees common to both our countries, including elm, alder, lime, hazel and poplar. My fondest memory of Euskadi is, of course, *Gernikako Arbola*, our Tree of Guernica.

Igandea, 1942 Urria 25

We're only getting two and a half pints of milk per week because of rationing. Doesn't go very far.

Igandea, 1942 Azaroa 15

All that beautiful wrought iron work sacrificed for the war effort. And hopefully one day soon, the swords will be turned back into ploughshares, and spears into sickles, as Isiah so cleverly puts it. Those low walls outside the church look defenceless now that the railings have been removed.

Asteartea, 1942 Abendua 1

This wartime coalition may seem quite draconian in its powers at times, but at least they're optimistic. And I don't think these lads will tolerate being told what to do by the Toffs once the war's over. Quite revolutionary thinking (despite banning the *Daily Worker*!). The Beveridge Report is taking a radical look at the impact of poverty on health and I think the policies that come out of it will be good for the poorer classes, providing a safety net. No longer having to find a few shillings to pay the doctor: the NHS is going to be free!

That should mean they'll present at our surgeries in good time rather than leaving it till the illness is beyond treatment. Free vitamins, cod liver oil, orange juice, milk, etc. And National Assistance will help those without a job. I may have to take on more staff if it's successful.

Asteazkena, 1942 Abendua 30

The insurance companies are up in arms! Their little scam is seriously under threat from Beveridge. 'Social Insurance', he calls it. Is no private industry safe from this man? Good on him, I say!

Igandea, 1943 Urtarrila 9

Atlético Bilbao beat Barcelona 2:1. We scored 3. Two by Elices, and the other was an own goal, early on, by Bertol.

Asteartea, 1943 Otsaila 2

German forces defeated by the weather in Stalingrad.

Astelehena, 1943 Martxoa 15

Franco's created the Blue Brigade to go and fight alongside the Germans in Leningrad. I suppose, in his mind, it's no different from fighting the Communists in Spain.

Asteakzkena, 1943 Apirila 21

Aberdeen took a real pounding from the Luftwaffe today. Never know which city they'll target next.

Asteakzena, 1943 Ekaina 30

The Germans have shot down a passenger plane over the Bay of Biscay. I imagine they thought Churchill was one of the passengers.

Larunbata, 1943 Uztaila 31

They've finally got Mussolini. He's been arrested. Gives me some hope that Franco will meet the same fate.

Igandea, 1943 Abutztua 15

So many illnesses affecting the lungs. If only we had a cure. Failing that, maybe prevention? But that would involve a huge education campaign, and, in any case, it's mainly attributable to poverty. If they can't afford to eat properly, or to heat their houses, what can we expect?

Ostirala, 1943 Iraila 3

Mussolini's tanks engage their legendary three reverse gears. Has Italy surrendered? The Allies are in the south, worried that if they see Naples, they might die. (*Vedi Napoli e poi muori!*) But you can't trust Benito. The Germans have saved him again. So, the North of Italy might take some small effort on our part to recover.

Igandea, 1943 Urria 31

At last, we have a cure for consumption! Streptomycin, the first antibiotic remedy for tuberculosis, has been produced by researchers at Rutgers University.

Isteguna, 1944 Otsaila 24

I love it when I hear songs in Spanish or Portuguese because they remind me of home. I hate Franco, but not the Spanish language. Just been listening to *Bésame Mucho* by Consuelo Velázquez. I also like *Inolvidable*, which was written by the Cuban pianist, Julio Gutiérrez.

Asteakzena, 1944 Martxoa 29

I took Ashlin to see *La torre de los siete jorobados* at the cinema. I think it helped her understand how difficult it is to follow the plot in a language you don't speak. There were no subtitles. 'Tower' and 'hunchback' were the only words she could work out.

Asteakzena, 1944 Maiatza 31

It's quite warm today. Officially, 91 degrees Fahrenheit. What I don't quite get is why the British measure temperatures in what looks like some German system. Apparently, to convert to centigrade, or Celsius, you need a degree in mathematics. I'd guess it's more than 30, even in the shade. That's going to give me some grief tomorrow when I get a whole new crop of patients with sunstroke. They just won't cover up. Ginger hair and pale skin is a recipe for disaster.

Asteartea, 1944 Ekaina 6

I don't understand: why's it called D-Day? Everybody seems to have a different theory. Debarkation? Designation? Douglas? Dwight? Deutschland? Or just misunderstanding a guy with a stutter? Maybe it means 'D' for day, nothing more sinister. Ultimately, it doesn't matter. This must be the turning point I keep longing for. The Germans are surely on the run!

Astelehena, 1944 Uztaila 12

Heard Billie Holiday's song *Strange Fruit* on the wireless today. I'm determined to get the book by Lillian Smith. Knowing what I know about Hitler's views on Negroes, I think it's my duty to challenge that nonsense about a ban on whites interbreeding with coloured folk.

Ostirala, 1944 Abuzua 25

Liberté, egalité, fraternité! Vive la France! At last, I can think of *etorkizunean* (the future) instead of living one day at a time. Time to start planning.

Larunbata, 1944 Urria 21

Now I see why there is such a shortage of doctors here in the UK. They've virtually all been drafted into the military to treat the casualties of war.

Larunbata, 1944 Abendua 16

They're defeated. Only a matter of time now. But the days pass so slowly. When will this all end? There's so much devastation here in Glasgow. How long will it take to reconstruct, assuming someone comes up with the money? And even when the people get rehoused, the war's not over, because the war in their heads will reverberate for years to come. So many broken bones and minds. Whatever can I do to help? Just heard that Glenn Miller died in an air crash.

Asteartea, 1945 Urtarrila 15

Los tres caballeros. I remember Disney's Mickey Mouse, but now he's got Donald Duck, and the cartoons in Spanish, too. Never trusted Disney. There seems to have been a lot of collusion between the different film studios.

Astelehena, 1945 Otsaila 19

And so, it continues. The Yanks take on the Japs and win. They need to establish a base so that they can launch an attack on the Japanese mainland. It's amazing how quickly we got the news. Reception's not brilliant on this radio with its accumulator and endless amount of aerial wire. And then there's that tricky bit trying to find the 'sweet spot' where I can hear the words long enough to catch the drift of what the newscaster is saying. Some would say this radio is the cat's whiskers! Useful to have a passing knowledge of other languages, too.

You can build up a picture of something approaching the truth from listening to the various sides. Even Lord Haw-Haw with his 'Germany calling, Germany calling' was entertaining, in an odd sort of way.

Osteguna, 1945 Martxoa 22

Looks like the Americans will be claiming it was they who won the war single-handedly. First Japan, now Germany. America, the world's policemen.

Osteguna, 1945 Apirila 12

Different president, different strategy, perhaps? Looks like Truman's getting impatient with the time it's taking to defeat Japan. Seems like he's also very suspicious of Stalin's motives. Probably right not to trust him. Weren't Uncles Joe and Adolf secretly planning their own allegiance in 1939? Something about carving up Poland between them? What a dangerous cocktail! A Molotov-Ribbentrop cocktail!

Astelehena, 1945 Apirila 30

Never a very satisfactory end, suicide. Leaves so many unanswered questions and a playground for speculation. I'd have liked to have seen Hitler in court, but of course, we would have executed him, anyway, eventually. "Why Guernica?" I'd have asked him. 'Just for fun', he'd probably have replied. 'Just target-practice, a rehearsal for the real theatre of war'.

Astelehena, 1945 Maiatza 7

I can't believe the Germans have surrendered. But it was on the BBC so it must be true. Maybe wait to see it in print? Tomorrow, perhaps? I fancy a trip to the cinema. Always makes more sense when you see the newsreels from Pathé.

Asteartea, 1945 Maiatza 8

Well, whilst D didn't seem to have a meaning, V. E. certainly does! They're out on the streets again in London, I hear. It's catching. Glasgow knows how to party, and doesn't the city deserve to dance after all this time playing hide-and-seek? It's like I remember *martes de Carnaval*. Lots of people are given a special dispensation by the government, no less, to throw off their inhibitions. I've never seen such gay abandon before in Scotland.

Ashlin, Asier, Jackie, John, VE Day

John Oswald's War Diary

By September 1940, the Royal Air Force had won the hard-fought Battle of Britain, downing hundreds of German bombers and fighters. Furiously, the Nazis turned their terror on major British cities.

One Saturday morning in summer, 1940, I had my first experience of aerial bombardment. A lone German plane launched a stick of bombs at the Clyde shipyards near my home at Scotstoun. The bombs fell on tenement buildings in nearby Langholm Street killing many civilians, mainly women and children. I watched as the rescuers removed the maimed and broken bodies of neighbours.

Soon after, I was called up. I was sent to Bletchley Park where I met Alan Turing (well I saw him from a distance).

Turing helped adapt a device originally developed in Poland

On the first day of the war, at the beginning of September 1939, Turing took up residence at Bletchley Park, the ugly Victorian Buckinghamshire mansion that served as the wartime HQ of Britain's top codebreakers. There he was a key player in the battle to decrypt the coded messages generated by Enigma, the German military's typewriter-like cipher machine. Some historians estimate that Bletchley Park's massive codebreaking operation, especially the breaking of U-boat Enigma, shortened the war in Europe by as many as two to four years.

My Bletchley experience was short-lived. No sooner had I arrived, I was shipped off to Spain to help keep an eye on Franco. I believe my experience in Guernica and my knowledge of Spanish had something to do with this. An officer sat me down to thrash out some ideas. "You have been chosen to travel to Spain. Be ready to ship out first thing tomorrow. Here are your orders," he said.

"Yes, Sir," I replied.

And so, I headed to Spain disguised as a Catholic priest. My best friend in Glasgow, Father George Gillespie, a Catholic priest, taught me all I know. My orders simply read, 'Mingle with all. Read all the newspapers. Our men will find you'. My travel instructions read, 'Don't be fucking late. Seamus'. I also had to mingle with officials and transmit radio messages to Gibraltar.

At first, I felt a little guilty, marrying (or not) dozens of young couples, baptising (or not) scores of babies, presiding over funerals, and saying mass. Everything was going well and after a while, I started to believe I was a priest. When I made it to Madrid, *Opus Dei* started sniffing around.

July 1940

I pondered to think what Franco would do with a Scottish *Protestant* spy disguised as a priest? It was time to get out of Madrid.

António de Oliveira Salazar in 1940

At first, I thought about heading to Portugal and the coast, but headed to Gibraltar instead.

Portugal in World War II was neutral, but Portuguese Prime Minister, António de Oliveira Salazar's, decision to stick with the oldest alliance in the world, cemented by the Treaty of Windsor (1386) between Portugal and England, which is still in force today, meant that the Anglo-Portuguese Alliance allowed Madeira to help the Allies. And in July 1940, around 2,000 Gibraltarian evacuees were shipped to Madeira. This was due to the high risk of Gibraltar being attacked by either Spain or Germany. The Germans had planned an attack and codenamed it Operation Felix, which was never started. It was time to contact Ashlin and Asier.

Just a quick note to let you know I am safe and well. I don't think I will be home until the war ends, but I can assure you I am in no immediate danger. I am learning new skills and have met a nice lady nurse. I know you will be really busy and dearly wish I could be with you.

God bless,

John

The Gibraltarians are fondly remembered on the island where they were called Gibraltinos. Some Gibraltarians married Madeirans during this time and stayed after the war was over. I did neither. I spent my time reporting daily via the radio, doing odd jobs, and playing the guitar. All the while, I knew Ashlin and Asier would be working their socks off. I would have been more of a use back home.

When the war ended, continued to see Jackie and went straight back to work on the Clydebank Press.

Monument to remember the Gibraltarian evacuees in Madeira.

The frustrating thing was I couldn't tell anyone what I had done during the war when I eventually got home. Part of me felt guilty. Part of me felt relieved. Part of me felt embarrassed. Part of me didn't know what to feel. I felt such a fraud. Everyone thought I was some sort of government super spy. One good thing to come out of my Madeira experience was meeting Scottish nurse, Jackie White. I returned home.

Post-War Diaries

Asier

Astertea, 1945 Ekaina 12

Life expectancy in Glaswegian men is just sixty-four. A safe assumption that they'll not live to claim a pension. 7% of the population suffers from T.B. Women can expect to live to sixty-eight. But infant mortality rates were horrendous. What a difference the new reservoir at Loch Katrine has made! That's better sanitation taken care of. But there are so many more things to do. Just look at the housing situation. It can't be healthy living in such cramped conditions. (The Church sees the latter as a threat to morals!)

Mostly, it's poverty at the root of it all. The authorities have not missed a trick: they show educational films alongside the main features at the local cinema. How can I persuade people to drink more milk? It's crucial for the development of healthy bones. And don't get me started on fruit and vegetables, they won't touch anything halfway healthy.

A typical family

Astelehena, 1945 Uztaila 26

Truly amazing. A socialist Labour government in the UK? I suppose there were signs that the Toffs had their day. Churchill must feel disgruntled, after he won the war for us. But I'm optimistic. I see determination in the hearts and minds of the men from the Clyde.

Astelehena, 1945 Abutzua 6

I just don't get it. Like Guernica. Only this time, it's the Americans. What's Truman up to? I reckon he saw this as a once-in-a-lifetime chance to try out his nuclear weapons with impunity. Something to do with stopping the war with Japan before Russia got in on the act. He doesn't trust Stalin, and neither does Churchill. This bomb was not necessary.

Osteguna, 1945 Abutzua 9

And another one! Was this inevitable? 'It will speed up the point at which the war comes to an end, and this will save lives in the long run'. Tell that to the innocent Japanese people. I'm sure they wouldn't understand how their sacrifice was just necessary collateral damage.

Igandea, 1945 Iraila 2

Surprise, surprise! The Japanese have surrendered. Faced with such overwhelming odds, what option did they have?

Igandea, 1945 Urria 14

I had the first decent night's sleep in what seems like an eternity. Nothing could have woken me up. A full twelve hours. And I didn't have nightmares this time. I dreamt of my beloved Euskadi with its long and proud traditions. Boys were playing *pelota*; young couples were eating *pintxos*; old men were wearing *txapelas*; bands were playing *dultzaina and txistu.*

Astelehena, 1945 Azaroa 5

Has the bombing started again? Of course, not! All I'm hearing is the fireworks. I'd forgotten about Guido Fawkes. The animals are scared, but the kids are enjoying the bonfire. There's real sense of community once again, now that people feel safe to venture outdoors. Our neighbours have baked some potatoes and there's gingerbread, too. Bottles of 'pop' for the kids.

Asteartea, 1945 Abendua 25

Izan gabe eman dezakegun gauza bakarra da zoriona (Happiness is the only thing we can give without having). It's the thought that counts. It seems that Christmas cards must be sent. A few presents for the children, yes. I bought some scent for Ashlin. Hard to know whether she appreciated it. I suppose she wouldn't want to offend me by saying it wasn't to her taste.

World War II Allies:

Winston Churchill

Born: 30 November 1874, Blenheim Palace, Woodstock; Died: 24 January 1965

Joseph Stalin

Born: 18 December 1878, Gori, Georgia
Died: 5 March 1953, Kuntsevo Dacha, Moscow, Russia

Franklin D Roosevelt

Born: 30 January 1882, Hope Park, New York, United States; Died: 12 April 1945, Warm Springs, Georgia, United States

Axis Powers:

The 'Tripartite Pact', also known as the 'Berlin Pact', was an agreement between Germany, Italy and Japan signed in Berlin on 27 September 1940 by Adolf Hitler, Galeazzo Ciano, and Saburō Kurusu.

Benito Mussolini

Born: 29 July 1883, Predappio, Italy
Died: 28 April 1945, Giulino, Italy

Adolf Hitler

Born: 20 April 1889, Braunau am Inn, Austria
Died: 30 April 1945, Berlin, Germany

Hideki Tojo

Born: 30 December 1884 Kōjimachi ward, Tokyo, Japan
Died: 23 December 1948, Tokyo, Japan

World War II was the deadliest military conflict in history in absolute terms of total dead: over 50 million people were killed.

1946-50: Francoist Spain is ostracised by United Nations and many countries sever diplomatic relations.

We must never forget. May the deeds of truly evil people be judged by a higher power and inspire future generations to live in peace and protest through debate and all forms of art.

James

Asier:

"My diary dates have become less regular, more intermittent since the war came to an end. I am also more able to understand the Glasgow vernacular."

Ashlin
1946

Is the war really over at long last? I suppose it must be: why else would the government be encouraging women to reconsider their function in society? It's quite subtle, actually. *Woman's Realm* magazine tells me my job now is to make my husband happy, and that includes mainly wifely chores around the house. I should be a good housewife. The fact that many women had to learn how to do men's work—agricultural and industrial work—just to keep the economy ticking over, whilst the men were away soldiering, seems to have been forgotten.

Any female who protests that she would be happy to continue in work is thought to be selfish: didn't we realise that the demobilised men must now take back the jobs they did before the war? A woman's place is in the home. And, by the way, there are babies to make! A baby boom was inevitable, bearing in mind the desires of all those sex-starved soldiers!

Asier
1946

Why not finish the job you started? Isn't it time to get rid of the remaining dictator? He'll never let go of power. Sanctions and the usual catalogue of diplomatic measures are like water off a duck's back. But no one here seems to care. So long as the Americans implement the Marshall Plan, Europe will be happy. Have they forgotten what Franco did? Doesn't the contamination from Germany make him just as dangerous as Hitler? I detect only a deafening silence from the Allies.

After a short baby boom, immediately after the war peaking in 1946, the United Kingdom experienced a second baby boom during the 1960s, with a peak in births in 1964, and a third, smaller boom peaking in 1990.

1947

Start of the NHS in Scotland

5 July 1948 is the official 'vesting' day of the National Health Service across the UK. In Scotland, the service was set up by a separate act passed in 1947.

These young hooligans. I mean the local teenage boys. Making a real nuisance of themselves. Petty crime everywhere. I put it down to the lack of a male role model in the home. This winter was a bad one for weather. 20 feet of snow, they say. And so damned cold. Doesn't help when we've run out of decent coal.

Ashlin

1947

Jesus and Mary, it's a cold winter! Luckily, I still have my personal hot water bottle substitute, if you know what I mean! It doesn't feel as if we've won the war, what with all the rationing still in place. Of course, shortages have encouraged a black market in scarce resources, with things like cigarettes being traded as if they were currency. And vulnerable folk are finding themselves pressurised into buying what are most likely stolen or contraband goods, either purely out of self-preservation or because if they didn't participate, the 'community' would send them to Coventry.

1948

NHS Established

The NHS was born on 5 July 1948 out of a long-held ideal that good healthcare should be available to all, regardless of wealth. When health secretary, Aneurin Bevan, opens Park Hospital in Manchester, it is the climax of a hugely ambitious plan to bring good healthcare to all. For the first time, hospitals, doctors, nurses, pharmacists, opticians and dentists are brought together under one umbrella organisation that is free for all at the point of delivery. The central principles were clear: the health service will be available to all and financed entirely from taxation, which means that people pay into it according to their means.

Asier
1948

Well, I don't know how to react to this. Britain has abolished judicial corporal punishment, at least birching and flogging. I think we'll have to keep it in schools just to instil some discipline. Good news, though.

They've set up the National Health Service! Great news for Ashlin and me. It's what we needed up here. You can't sell a service to people who can't afford to pay. The only such service I know of is a funeral service, where the family usually ends up paying the bill.

Asier and a neighbour

Ashlin
1948

I never thought I'd praise politicians, but this new National Health Service is going to be a godsend for the impoverished people of Glasgow. At least, Asier won't have to deliberate whether to charge his patients or waive the fee, because now, everyone is entitled to treatment free of charge. Coupled with this, the Labour government has got brilliant plans for re-housing folks from the slums.

Ashlin
1949

I don't know what to make of what the Allies have done with Germany. Someone must have thought that carving it up into four sections would stop the country ever getting ideas about future imperialism. Russia wanted the bit that included Berlin, and the Western Allies weren't having that. Dropping supplies into the capital was an amazing feat.

Asier
1949

It's good that we could help the Germans in Berlin. Yes, I suppose with the passage of time I've forgiven them. I've started to re-examine my attitude towards the Russians, though. Without the airlift, many Berliners would have starved to death.

Ashlin
1950

We're seeing a lot of patients recently who are, in their words, 'bad with their nerves'. Some of them are ex-servicemen, but others are civilians, amongst them many women. Not much we can do for them, quite honestly, short of locking them away, but what good would that do? But at least, we now recognise 'shell-shock' and the like. During the Great War, many soldiers were shot for what was seen as cowardice.

John
1950

Working-class families were very fastidious, on the whole. Much of this pride in one's appearance went hand-in-hand with church-going, with families believing that: 'Cleanliness is next to Godliness!'. Shaming was the main weapon against slovenliness as communities had to share amenities such as outdoor toilets, and wouldn't tolerate any individual who stepped out of line. One positive outcome of residents' regular use of powerful disinfectants was to help keep germs at bay. But it wasn't just about health issues: the front door step was scrubbed to within an inch of its life and whitened, using pipe clay.

This was a very bold statement: it implied that the interior of the house was similarly immaculate. Any brassware had to be polished until you could see your face in it. It was very much about 'keeping up appearances'. The best china, if you had any, was kept for special occasions, and some items were so special they never saw the light of day.

Working-class trades were highly respected and great pride was taken in seeing a young apprentice progress to journeyman. Even the police were somewhat reluctant to proceed when they realised that the man they were expected to challenge about what was seen as antisocial behaviour at the time was a miner, for example. As the men in families became proficient at working in brass, you would find them turning their hands to forging brass items for the home.

(As burglary, and crime in general, were a rare occurrence at the time, at least within working-class communities, brass knuckle-dusters were rarely to be found, however!) To save money, men would usually have a *last* so that they could repair the family's shoes. Equally, the pudding basin was often taken out so that no one ever had to visit the barber.

There was a clear delineation between what was seen as the man's sphere of influence and that of the woman. Though her place may have been in the home, she was the queen there, and woe betide any man who dared to cross the line! She baked cakes and produced *cloutie dumplings*, as well as often quite nutritious soups. She did the cooking, so any would-be male chef was taunted with being a big 'Jessie'. (Men were occasionally allowed, and sometimes expected, to contribute to Sunday meals, however). Technical jobs, such as changing the gas mantle, were generally left to the men.

Asier
1950

There's a real witch-hunt going on in America. McCarthy's got a thing about Communists. He sees 'reds under the beds' everywhere, but particularly in the entertainment industry. Right and left-wing politics have got so polarised now, I seriously must ask myself where I stand. I thought I knew when I was an idealistic young man. Now I'm not so certain.

Ashlin
1951

I don't know what science is coming to! Contraceptive pills? That's going to be a real moral dilemma for me, quite honestly. Father O'Brian always used to tell couples to learn to curb their desires, if they wanted to limit the number of children they would have. Even then he maintained that 'God will provide' regardless of the number of children you have. Try telling that to the poor Glaswegians who have barely two halfpennies to rub together.

'A woman's work is never done!' used to be the lament of many a matriarch. How any woman managed to find the time to do part-time jobs is anathema. A certain day was always reserved for doing the washing, usually Monday, and of course, this had to be agreed between all the residents in the close so that it didn't clash with someone else deciding to have a bonfire. Washing-day was really hard work, with chores made only marginally less onerous through the use of *mangles*, which squeezed out most of the moisture.

Some women would even push a pram load of washing across the town to the local *steamie,* more to hear the local gossip, it would seem. Carpets were hung over the line and beaten to remove the dust.

Taking a bath was a rare occurrence, as it was so dependent on having enough hot water, but in larger families, the bath was dragged to its place in front of the fire, with family members taking turns as the water got progressively dirtier, though it was kept warm by adding pans of hot water. Not surprisingly, many preferred the public baths. Some people had a *geyser* which produced a dribble of hot water, though hardly enough for a bath.

Asier

Churchill's back in power. Luis E. Miramontes has invented a contraceptive pill that women can take orally. This goes against my religion but I can understand how it might enable some of the women Ashlin sees to escape the poverty trap. Can't help wondering if women will live to regret succumbing to this unnatural process, maybe repercussions down the line that the medics have not anticipated?

Ashlin
1952

It's a strange fact that people only appreciate the value of something when they have to pay for it. Even a nominal charge seems essential, otherwise the free vitamins often go unused.

People are funny. Take my brother, John, for instance. Sometimes I just wish he would challenge me occasionally instead of going along with everything I tell him to do. Now Asier, on the other hand, there's a man who knows his own mind, and I admire that in a man.

Asier
1952

When I write prescriptions, they will cost the patient one shilling. You must charge something for them. Otherwise, people just don't appreciate what they're getting. I've noticed that, when Ashlin hands out the free vitamins. I'm getting to like her very much. I'd find her rather bossy if I were in her brother's shoes. John does as he's told. I seem to command a little more respect, to be honest.

Ashlin
1953

'The King is dead! Long live the Queen!' I've been left to man the fort, whilst my boys go off to the shipyards for the launch of the royal yacht. I hope they take some snaps of Her Majesty whilst they're down there. Might be some time before she's back here again.

Asier
Osteguna, 1953 Martxoa 5

Stalin is dead. Where there's death, there's hope!

The UK has a new queen, and as if to mark the occasion, she's just launched the Royal Yacht Britannia at John Brown Shipbuilders in Clydebank. John and I went down there to watch. We were each given a paper union flag to wave. It reminds me of the design of the Basque flag.

1954

I'm sad to say that it's probably true that there's a link between smoking and lung cancer. I know we doctors used to turn a blind eye to smoking. We thought, during the war, that it calmed the nerves—probably, on balance, the lesser of two evils, at the time. Oh, and Churchill's still in office at the age of eighty! Must be some kind of a record.

Ashlin
1954

They say smoking's bad for you, but it does calm the nerves. I should know, I get through quite a few myself. Of course, as a woman, I couldn't be seen to be smoking in public, and especially not a woman of my social standing. But it does look quite 'cool', as they say, when you see female film stars with their cigarette holders, and then there's that hint of *romance* as the male lead offers them a light from his gold cigarette lighter.

1955

Not sure about whether television will catch on. I prefer the radio because you can have it playing in the background whilst you get on with your chores. Too much of a distraction, I would say, television.

Asier
1955

Billy Graham's here in Scotland, evangelising. You'd think from his propaganda that the only God-fearing people in the world come from America. Does he think the Scots are all heathens?

Spain has been allowed to join the United Nations. I can't see Franco being removed from power anytime soon.

Ashlin
1956

I'd forgotten how much we used to enjoy our trips to the seaside as kids. As the weather looked promising, Asier and I went off to Saltcoats for the day. What fun we had! I even removed my stockings and went paddling in the sea. Asier enjoyed an ice-cream and a fish supper.

Asier
1956

No proven link between smoking and lung cancer, they say. However, there's one silver lining in the clouds: The Clean Air Act has been introduced. By controlling the burning of coal with a high sulphur content, we may now see the last of smog in the cities. I'm sure the air pollution is at least as bad for us all as smoking.

1957

Foot and Mouth Disease has been found at an abattoir in Liverpool. That'll be bad news for the farmers who'll be forced to slaughter many of their herds of cows. I remember going down to see some jazz performers at the Cavern Club in Liverpool. My kind of music!

Ashlin

1957

There's nothing better than a ceilidh for cheering you up in my opinion. The three of us played our usual eclectic mix of musical styles, and folk just got up and danced, whether they had two left feet or not, though most of us, being Catholic, were doubly blessed!

1958

We all attended Midnight Mass together this year. They've added an extra public holiday this year: Christmas Day. Asier thinks we should celebrate the Adoration of the Magi, too, like they do in his country on 6 January.

7 Love and Loss

John Oswald's Guernica

Jackie was a godsend. In the past, I had always bottled up my feelings and found it hard to talk about emotions. But with Jackie it was different. She put me totally at ease. I could talk to her about anything. The fact that she was totally gorgeous helped too. When I returned from the war, Ashlin and Asier had become close through work and were now sharing a bed.

Jackie lived in Edinburgh with her mum, dad, and brother. It took a while to convince her to move to Glasgow. In time, she moved into the big house in Victoria Park Drive North and the trio, Asier, Ashlin, and myself became four. Jackie got a job as a community nurse.

Together, we got up to all sorts of mischief. We went to concerts. We went dancing. We stayed up playing music all night. Sometimes in the house. Sometimes on the banks of Loch Lomond. And sometimes in church halls.

There were plans for a new housing complex across from the surgery. Six high-rise blocks were being built and Asier and Ashlin planned to build a new surgery on the estate with more services. On April's Fool Day, I may up a poster and put it up on the wall of their Dumbarton Road surgery. It read:

Dear People, We are considering moving across the road to larger premises, with more facilities and staff. If you agree, please fill in a verbal agreement form and hand it in to the surgery. You can pick one up at the post office. Just ask the postmaster.

The next day, the postmaster popped into the surgery and looked at the poster. He laughed and brought it to the attention of Ashlin. "I'll kill him," she said.

"I think we both know who is responsible," said the postmaster. They took it down and had a good laugh.

Ashlin and Jackie had a lot in common through nursing, fashion and a love of books; for Asier and I, it was walking, talking, cooking, football and fishing. We all went everywhere together and had so much fun.

I will always remember the day I introduced Jackie to my best friend, Father George Gillespie. He wasn't your run of the mill Catholic priest: Rangers-daft, smoked like a chimney, owned a motorbike (with side-car) and conducted his sermons like a stand-up comedy routine. As a Protestant, Celtic fan, I only attended his masses for entertainment purposes and to play cards with George afterwards.

I think some of the spiritual things stuck with me though. Jackie was a devout Catholic and didn't know what to expect.

"So, this is the fine lady who has ruined my social life?" George said.

"So, you are the rascal that trained John on all things priestly. Giving him the powers to snare me in a trap, like a helpless bunny," said Jackie. George and I looked at each other.

"Eh, we can't talk about official government business," we both said in unison.

George then took us for a run on his motorbike to Loch Lomond, stopping off at the big house for picnic supplies. We sat by the Bonnie Banks for hours telling stories of days gone by. George even talked Jackie into doing readings at mass. It was a brilliant. A summer's day spent in one of the most idyllic locations on the planet, with my girlfriend and best friend. Jackie fell pregnant just before the new surgery was opened in Kingsway Court.

The four of us agreed to turn the old surgery into a home for Jackie and me. It was beautiful. We had a yellow nursery complete with drawers, a small wardrobe, toys and a Moses basket. The big room was for Jackie and me and the smaller room was turned into office space. The lounge faced on to Kingsway Court and rickety old trams on Dumbarton Road.

Jackie had kept well all through the pregnancy. We knew she was having twins and Asier and Ashlin checked in on her regularly. 1957 was coming to an end and we spent Hogmanay with Asier and Ashlin on Victoria Park Drive North. Next day, after dinner, we decided to walk home through the park. When we got back to the flat, Jackie collapsed. I lifted her onto our bed and asked a neighbour to go and fetch Asier and Ashlin.

Within two hours, I was sitting by her bed in the Western Infirmary. The doctors were talking and I had no idea what was going on. After a while, Ashlin and Asier explained to me that they had to deliver the babies as quickly as possible. And that Jackie might not survive. Or I could lose the Jackie and babies. I was devastated. I couldn't imagine life without Jackie and I certainly didn't have the skills to bring up babies on my own. "Try to save them all, but please, I beg of you, do your best," I cried.

The twins were born on 3 January 1958. We named the boys James and John (Julio). Jackie slowly faded away five days later. I could stay with her and at the very least we had time to say goodbye. "If you are ever faced with the dilemma of saving me or the boys again, promise me you will save the boys," said Jackie.

I knew Jackie didn't have long to go, though I didn't fully understand why. Maternal death they call it. All I kept thinking was why? This is so unfair. The doctors and nurses made her as comfortable as possible. She looked beautiful. Almost angelic. Ashlin and Ashlin were with me when she passed. Right up until her last breath, she was still talking about the good time we all had together. I couldn't let go of her hand for more than an hour after her death. Ashlin and Asier took me home that night and gave me some medication to ease the pain.

The next day, I walked to what was supposed to be me and Jackie's and new home. It was perfect, except no Jackie. I stayed for a week, cried my eyes out, got completely drunk and ate little or no food. It was then that Asier came to my rescue. "Do you remember when I was ready to end it all in Guernica," he said.

"I think so," I replied.

"Well, this is *your* Guernica. And with the right help and support, you will get through this. Believe me, I know. This time will pass. And didn't Jackie tell you to take care of the boys?"

"Yes, but how," I replied.

"We will take care of the funeral and all of the arrangements. We understand if you feel you can't attend. I have been talking to your friend, George Gillespie. He knows a place on Millport you can go to. Once you are on the mend, we can all decide what's best for the twins."

"When do I leave?" I replied.

"Tomorrow. George will take you down," he said.

For the next year, I became the odd jobs man in a Catholic church on Millport. In the Roman Catholic Church, the Seal of Confession (or Seal of the Confessional) is the absolute duty of priests not to disclose anything that they learn from penitents during the course of the Sacrament of Penance. I decided to take advantage of this and told the three priests on the island all about my wartime exploits.

They all just laughed and made jokes about it, asking me if I wanted to say mass or the odd wedding. The priests gave me simple accommodation, good food, company and a welcome routine. These guys really knew what they were doing. We had countless talks, walks and dinners. My soul was being strengthened and I didn't even know it. They would also take me fishing and encourage me to cycle around the island and tend the garden. "You must take care of your mental, physical, social, emotional, and spiritual health in equal measure," said Father Benny.

Give me physical pain any day of the week. I've never known anything like this: most of the time I just want to curl up and die. Asier put me on medication before travelling to Millport and showed me how to use it wisely. Attending mass helped too. This brought me closer to Jackie and George and gave me strength. Every week, I would exchange letters with Ashlin. She would tell me how the boys were, all the local gossip and how Asier and George were doing.

The post office on Millport was run by Lawrence and Lorraine O'Neill and over time, I became very friendly with this couple.

They were desperate for a child. After a long discussion with Asier and Ashlin, I asked the O'Neills to adopt James on the condition I could visit often, allow his brother to do the same, and let him know who his biological father was on his eighteenth birthday. They agreed. I then asked Ashlin and Asier to adopt John (later Julio).

After around eighteen months, I returned to the Clydebank Press on a part-time basis. I moved in with Asier and Ashlin and they devised a healthy routine for me. This included taking Julio for long walks in the healing grounds of Victoria Park.

Healing

Ashlin

1958

Mothers would remain in the home every day (I loved being with our new addition). How else would they have been able to address the requirements of sundry visitors during the day? There was the gas-man who came to read the metre; the coalman; the insurance man; the milkman; the list is endless. Children were often sent out to get a loaf of bread from the baker's: "Here's four pence-farthing, son!" When the horn or buzzer sounded at the factory, it meant 'knocking-off time', and women knew their husbands would be home shortly.

For men, being made 'idle' was not only a major stigma in being unemployed: there was also the greater fear of being sent to the poorhouse, like the one at Barnhill, just to get a few shillings to support your family. Shopping was seen as the province of women, who bought the family's clothing, including that of their husband. Men found the very idea of stepping into a shop intimidating or demeaning, or both. They might be called upon to cast their expert eye when a big item, such as a carpet, is purchased. 'Best Axminister, that one!'. Women didn't attend the cemetery after a funeral: that was the men's preserve.

John is coming home and we are adopting Julio. I am so excited.

John
1958

The priests in Millport have done a great job. I finally feel as though I can breathe. Faith is such a big part of health and I have decided to become a Catholic. My big mate, Father George (the mad Rangers supporter), will laugh his socks off. For years, I've been referring to him as an Irish Tattie Muncher.

Asier
1958

Although I prefer celebrating epiphany, I find it strange that this is the first year that Christmas Day has been officially recognised as a public holiday, here in Scotland. Of course, it's the New Year that's more important around here. We made our own amusement. Whether that was games such as ludo or snakes and ladders for the children, or musical interludes for the adults. An instrument was either passed down from father to son, or acquired very cheaply from the pawn shop in preparation for 'a bit of a do'. The usual decorum was suspended at certain times of the year, notably Hogmanay, when greater than average quantities of alcohol were imbibed which gave rise to ribald jokes and innuendo.

1959

I know a lot of people who own cars nowadays. A few have televisions, too.

On the health front, I'm pleased to see a new Mental Disorders Act. At least, we don't have to label people as *cretins* or *moral imbeciles* any more. An acknowledgement that it's got nothing to do with a perceived lack of intelligence. I've come across cases where kids have ended up in institutions just because they were born out of wedlock.

Ashlin
1959

I'm so pleased Asier can drive. That really opens up possibilities at weekends. Before, we were totally dependent on public transport to get us around. I'd love to learn to drive, but people around here would regard that as a somewhat frivolous ambition: why ever would a woman need to drive?

Asier

1960

In the 1960 European Cup Final at Hampden Park on 18 May, Real Madrid. Beat Eintracht Frankfurt 7:3. It was, for me, not only an exciting game with lots of action, but also one where I could not decide who I least wanted to lose (the Germans or Franco's Real Madrid!).

Ashlin

1960

Up until quite recently, there was thought to be very little difference between people with learning disabilities and those with classic mental illnesses. Both groups were deemed to lack capacity and needed the state to make decisions on their behalf. Now that we have the Mental Disorders Act, there is a perceived acknowledgement that mental illness has nothing to do with the results of IQ tests that are used to label various categories of human beings in the most disparaging terms.

John

1961

It's great being home. The old trio back together with baby Julio tagging along for the ride. We all decided to change his name to Julio, John. Asier said it would look better if he got to play for the Spanish football team.

Asier

1961

Enoch Powell, the UK Health Minister, has just approved providing the contraceptive pill on the NHS. Given his views on race, I dare say he'll regret limiting the number of children white families are likely to have in the future! The young women of the late sixties heard the pill discussed in the news and read about it in magazines and newspapers. But officially, it was not for us. It came to the UK in 1961, but as in the US, was available only to married women on prescription.

Ashlin

1961

The contraceptive pill has just been approved for use in the UK. The NHS will provide it free of charge. I can't help imagining that the Tories have a hidden agenda. Do they just want the plebs to use it to stop them 'breeding like rabbits'? It reminds me a bit of Aldous Huxley's *Brave New World* where successive generations are bred purely and simply to match the jobs and skills required by the state.

Asier

1962

RNA and DNA. Sounds fascinating. Wonder what the implications will be for science and medicine?

Why are they getting rid of all the trams and trolley buses? Glasgow will be the last tram system to go. Now all we have is left is those running up and down the coast at Blackpool, like some kind of museum piece.

John

1962

Ashlin and Asier had a small private wedding this year. Big George handled the ceremony and I was the best man.

I have gone back to work full-time. Big Josie has redecorated the community flat and passed all of Jackie's clothes on to other women. I sometimes spend the odd weekend there. I think we will rent it out until we decide what we're going to do with it.

Ashlin

1962

Though I do like the radio, the BBC's beginning to sound rather upper class, insisting, as it does, that all their presenters use 'received pronunciation'. It sounds even more ridiculous when some ageing disc jockey announces a track by the Beatles, or worse still, the Rolling Stones. Are we hastening the demise of public transport by driving our own vehicles, and is this letting the side down in respect of our working-class roots or should we be more aspirational and insist on our right to own cars, just like the rich?

Asier

1963

There seems to be an ideological urge on the part of the Conservatives to destroy most of public transport: first the trams and trolley buses, and now Beeching's shutting down much of the railway network. Meanwhile, motorway construction is thriving. Do they really believe that every family in the country will have a car? Ominously, Hitler did: that was the origin of the Volkswagen (the ordinary people's car).

1964

Outrageous in this day and age! A typhoid epidemic in Aberdeen. They've had to close all the schools.

Picasso has just shown his *Tête d'homme barbu à la cigarette II*. That's nearly thirty years since he painted *Guernica*.

Ashlin

1964

You think modern medicine has eliminated many diseases, but then, suddenly, along comes an outbreak of typhoid in Aberdeen. Are the doctors too complacent or arrogant in thinking they have got major illnesses under control? Maybe it's better housing, better sanitation, better nutrition and better education that have brought about increased longevity in the population.

Asier

1965

They're finally completing the trials of the Germans who ran the concentration camps. It's taken twenty years!

Churchill dies on 24 January 1965

Igandea, 1965 Urtarrila 24

Churchill is dead. He was a hero for many.

Ashlin

1965

I must admit that now we have commercial television alongside the BBC, it does feel like it belongs to us. They speak our language. They don't talk down to us. On the other hand, there are all those annoying advertisements, but it does give you the time to make a cup of tea.

1966

As a matter of principle, Asier and John refuse to watch the World Cup Final between England and Germany. All I heard was: 'They think it's all over, it is now!'. When two tribes go to war...

Asier

1966

The Spanish government has forbidden British military aircraft from overflying Spain. It's been a long while since I heard any news about Spain. Maybe Franco doesn't like Harold Wilson's Labour government?

1967

Thalidomide. Promised so much and yet delivered misery on a huge scale. At least some people are being held to account for it but these children will be disfigured for life.

1968

Spain has won the Eurovision Song Contest; seriously? Massiel, who won with the song *La, la, la*, beating the British pop singer Cliff Richard's *Congratulations*. The more I hear about this programme, the more I think it's a fix. A way to boost the Spanish economy, I would think. Franco wouldn't have let her sing it in her native Catalan, of course.

1969

Franco's a busy man these days. He's handed back some territory to Morocco. He's declared martial law in Spain and closed off the border with Gibraltar. Prince Juan Carlos is to be his successor.

Fermín Monasterio Pérez has been assassinated by ETA. I do hope this feud will end when a change of government in Spain finally comes.

1970

ETA kidnapped the German citizen, Eugen Beihl, in San Sebastián, but they later released him. In Burgos, 16 Basque terrorism suspects were tried. The Spanish government declared a three-month martial law in the Basque county of Guipuzco, because of strikes and demonstrations. 3 Basques were sentenced to death and 12 others were sentenced to imprisonment for up to sixty-two years. In Viscaya, 15,000 workers went on strike in protest at the death sentences. As a result, Franco commuted the sentence to thirty years in prison.

Ashlin

1970

It's strange how people change. Fashion seems to have an impact on everyone. Men included. I never thought I'd see Asier and John wearing their hair long, like the Beatles, but I suppose we all need to fit in and not be regarded as 'squares'. I too have started to wear increasingly shorter skirts. They say it's women's liberation; I'm not so sure about that!

Asier

1971

Decimalisation, they call it. I think it's just inflation by the back door. Maybe it's all part of gearing the UK up to join the Common Market? I attended a remembrance service in George Square, Glasgow. I also visited a monument for those who died in the Spanish Civil War in Glasgow.

Ashlin

1971

Precisely at the point when Asier was coming to terms with our, for him, complicated system of measurements, they have to bring in *decimalisation*! But some weren't happy with the new penny, so they introduced the *fractional* coin, the halfpenny!

Asier

1972

A Japanese soldier, Shoichi Yokoi, has been discovered in Guam. He had spent twenty-eight years in the jungle thinking Japan was still at war with the Allies!

Ashlin

1972

Why won't people acknowledge the effectiveness of mass immunisation? Don't they realise that for the herd to be protected, everyone has to be vaccinated?

Asier

1973

ETA has assassinated Luis Carrero Blanco, the Spanish Prime Minister, in Madrid.

Picasso has also passed away this year.

Ashlin

1973

Asier's very keen on what he calls 'green' solutions to environmental problems. He says it comes as second nature to him having been brought up in Euskadi. He's taken a keen interest in solar power, wind turbines and heat pumps. All beyond me!

Asier

1974

Well, I am surprised! The UK's had to switch to a three-day working week (to save energy). Reminds me of home: *Astelehena* is the first day of the week; *Asteartea* is the middle day of the week; *Asteazkena* is the last day of the week. After that comes the day after the week is over (Osteguna). They seem to have a similar story in Gaelic.

Incidentally, I was asking a local Gaelic speaker if his language had a word that would translate the Spanish word *mañana* which has a laidback sort of feel about it. He thought for a while and then replied: "Oh, no, we've nothing as urgent as that."

When introduced on the NHS, the pill was prescribed mainly to older women who already had children and did not want any more. The government at the time did not want to be seen to be encouraging promiscuity or 'free love'.

Although there were not any restrictions on its use, the take-up of GPs prescribing it was slow. That all changed in 1974 when family planning clinics could prescribe single women with the pill—a controversial decision at the time.

Many people had questions about whether GPs and parents had to be told when a young woman was prescribed the pill.

Ashlin

1974

Rationing has started again. This time we're being given petrol coupons. A three-day week and everyone's on strike.

1975

Franco is dead. We're going back to Spain to 'celebrate'. I'm so excited. Asier's taking me back to his former home. We're going by aeroplane. A new experience for us both.

9 Homeward Bound

Franco dies on 20 November 1975

Asteazkena, 1975 Azaroa 20

Ever since I heard that Franco was dead, I've been having an internal wrestling match with myself. Would I be safe now? Could I go back to Euskadi without taking the risk of someone identifying me as a war criminal? "Don't be so silly!" Ashlin says. "You're no war criminal. Faced with a scenario where it was either kill or be killed, you had no alternative. It was war. And anyway, I'm sure no one would recognise you now, after all this time. You were still a young man back then, and now look at you, a spritely pensioner, no less."

Maybe I should confront my fears. Realistically speaking, it's either now or never. Few people realise what it's like to be an *Glasgo*, a political exile. Imagine being rendered homeless by a sudden flood, or kicked out of your lodgings by an unscrupulous landlord. There you have it in a nutshell. A genuine loss of identity. A sense of displacement. But add to that, being forced to communicate through a language that is not your own; add to that being obliged to replace your native culture with an alien one.

Anyway, to cut a potentially very long story short, Ashlin finally convinces me to side with that part of me that is brave enough to take on my pilgrimage back to the Basque Country, naturally accompanied and supported by her.

I am surprised how easy it has become to travel to Spain. Thinking back to my relentless journeying by ship and train up to Glasgow, I wonder how I managed to survive. So, this time we take a plane, and before we know it, there we are in a newly liberated Spain. Let's go straight back to Guernica, I think, but Ashlin persuades me to show her some of the other attractions in Euskadi first.

Of course, though much *hasn't* changed, some of the features of the towns I knew so well are alien to me, and I'm consequently practically useless as her would-be guide. Right in the centre of Vitoria-Gasteiz, we see a gigantic tree. It's much taller now than when I last saw it back in the 1930s. It's a sequoia tree.

Must be at least 30 metres high, and its girth would be upwards of 7 metres, I would say. Even my own 'Tree of Guernica', planted nearly forty years ago, in a park just outside Glasgow is dwarfed by this tree.

As far as I can remember, the sequoia was planted over one hundred years ago. Nice to see continuity triumphing over what is seen as convenience. It is not always in the best interests of the community that the traditional must make way for modernity.

As we follow the Pilgrim's Way, we pass through the streets of Vitoria, and I am reassured to see the old guys still wearing their traditional berets. We stop at a small tapas bar and I order *pintxos* in Basque. It's all beginning to come back to me. You never forget the language you grew up speaking. A tram glides by and I look around at the municipal buildings. It's starting to feel so familiar. We go for a walk up in the town centre. The locals call this part the Almond because of its shape. After quite a climb, we turn around to look back over Vitoria. It is beautiful. It's Easter, but there is still snow on the hills, not far away.

Before we contemplate visiting Guernica, Ashlin insists that I take her to San Sebastian, or Donostia as I prefer to call it. As luck would have it, the weather is ideal and we take the bus. On arrival, I'm immediately bowled over by the amazing blue colour everywhere I look. And, wow, what's that I see fluttering in the trees? It's my beloved Basque flag. I'll try to describe it for you. Imagine, if you will, the Union Jack (or Union Flag, if you insist). If you replace the English element (the red cross) with a white cross and the white Scottish cross with a green cross, you're nearly there. All that remains is the background colour, which is red.

As we walk around the bay, we see memorials to earlier battles, and canons point proudly out to sea.

But now, I have reached the point of no return. Tomorrow, we head off to Guernica. I had thought we would have been able to take the train, but apparently not. We must travel first by bus to Bilbao, and then get another bus out to Guernica. Bilbao still looks impressive and had we planned our trip more carefully, we could have spent some time there, but our destination has to be Guernica. The bus journey is interesting and I listen to the familiar sounds of the Basque language emanating from my fellow passengers. But I don't attempt to engage them in conversation. My mind is on other things.

Ashlin rouses me from my reveries. "Look, Asier!" She exclaims, "The Germans are here!"

I don't know if she intended to frighten me but it certainly had that effect. We were just coming into Guernica, and sure enough, there was the Volkswagen garage on the approach. I had to remind myself that there was nothing sinister going on here but I was clearly having flashbacks to traumatic memories from forty years ago. We got off the bus, and the first thing I noticed was the railway line. It was right there that the German bombs had fallen. Little sign of a railway station now. We crossed the road.

I casually glanced at my watch, which conveniently had the date displayed. It was 26 April. Shivers ran down my spine. As I made my way towards the Tree of Guernica, I was aware of a crowd of people surrounding a man who didn't look like a local. Indeed, he was not. This was the son of George Steer who had made an annual pilgrimage to this place for as long as people could remember. He was honouring one of the many journalistic achievements of his father, who practically alone had highlighted what had happened in Guernica through the medium of *The Times*.

But, as I entered the museum, I tried to learn to forgive the German nation, even though Herzog, the then German President, was not to admit to German involvement in the attack on Guernica until 1998. Some accommodation had obviously been reached between public officials of our two countries which had led to Guernica being twinned with Pforzheim. It was all coming back to me now. Obviously, there had been some attempt to reconstruct Guernica as it had been, but, as elsewhere in the world, some new edifices had emerged out of the ashes, some barely distinguishable from other modern European cities. Call me old-fashioned, if you like, but I much prefer the earlier architecture.

The old *estacion de ferrocarril* was gone, but the railway remained. Buses seemed to be the transport of choice nowadays, though, of course, there were far more cars than I ever remember. I made my way to the *Casa de Juntas*, in existence for over five hundred years, and I experienced a sense of continuity and stability. Looking at that gift from José Antonio Aguirre (my father's watch), I am reminded of the inscription: *To Steer from the Basque Republic*. The *Casa de Juntas* was where, in October 1936, José Antonio Aguirre was elected the first President of Euskadi.

A similar sensation was provoked in me by the Tree of Guernica, immortalised in the song, written in 1853, which became a kind of nationalist anthem for us. The longevity experienced by a tree symbolises for me the fact that though mankind may come and go, nature will continue regardless. Like the tree, the Basque nation will also survive. Back in Scotland, my own Tree of Guernica is now thirty-eight years old. How time flies!

I was in awe as I wandered around inside the *Sala de Juntas*, all too conscious of the momentous decisions that had been taken here over the centuries. This was reinforced by the vast library of books displayed around the walls, the ornate seats and the religious figures and tradesmen depicted everywhere you looked. I felt so proud to be a Basque citizen once again.

Now that's quite something. There are some things bombs can't destroy. They can't destroy tradition and culture. Here's a statue of the man who wrote the song, *Tree of Guernica*. And over there is the actual tree! Dare I speak to the locals? I'll try. It goes well. I enquire about the tree. "Oh, don't you remember?" The old lady says. "The tree remains for as long as it is still growing but then gets replaced when it starts to die off. Continuity is thus assured." It's all very reassuring.

"What did she say?" Ashlin asks, and I realise I'm going to have to start translating everything for her.

We move on. It was all coming back to me now. And look, yes, there was the Church of Santa Maria, restored to its former glory. They must have rebuilt it after the bombing. Some things must be prioritised. "Stand over there, by the door," says Ashlin, and I duly comply, as she takes a photograph. She takes another of me alongside the Tree of Guernica. All down this street, there are trees, but they have had their branches lopped off to such an extent that they look more like statues.

We enter the Parliament Building. The wow-factor is indescribable. The ceiling is made up of a stained-glass image of the Tree of Guernica, symbolically meaning that parliament continues to meet under the tree, as it has since time immemorial.

We proceed to the museum, where they have attempted to re-create the sheer devastation of that day in 1937. The black-and-white photographs, some of them more like sepia in colour, serve to emphasise that this all happened decades ago, long before we used colour film. We note the valiant attempts by the British journalist, George Steer, to draw the attention of the world to this unforgivable violation, which seemed to fall on the deaf ears of the British Establishment, preoccupied as they were at the time by what they saw as potential threats from Communism, as opposed to the imminent threats from Fascism.

The Gernika Peace Museum, formerly known as the Gernika Museum, was founded on 7 April 1998.

The museum may be considered as a history museum in the sense that it was used as a guide to the history of Gernika-Lumo and, more particularly, to the Civil War and the bombing.

From 1999 to 2002, the museum carried out adaptation work on the building. A musicographic project was drawn up and carried through, and the decision was taken to turn the museum into a peace museum (the first peace museum in the Basque Country and the entire Spanish state). The Gernika Peace Museum has been a foundation since July 2002, with founder trustees the Basque Government, the *Diputación* or Provincial Council of Bizkaia, and Gernika-Lumo Town Hall. And so, the museum opened again on 8 January 2003 with a revamped profile and a wider range of possibilities.

It is now an institution in tune with the needs of our world today. The museum has grown into an attractive, dynamic space, a place where visitors may feel and live out a scenario in which history is taken by emotions and empathy to clear the path towards reconciliation, a place where we may think that we can all work together to shape our own peace.

Whilst human beings die in a bombing raid, inanimate objects survive, and in the museum, we see quite a few of these. Here were some playing cards, and over there some binoculars. There were personal documents as well as a typewriter and some discarded cigarette packets. Comparing the photographs taken just after the bombings with similar shots from the same angles taken today, we could see the level of total devastation that had been wrecked by the Luftwaffe.

We saw a café called Asier's and we went in. I was gratified to see Picasso's painting right there where it should be in the form of a mural. *Gernika*, as we refer to it in Basque. But I was ill-prepared for what was about to happen.

"Time for a coffee," said Ashlin.

"Where did you get the name for the café?" Ashlin asked.

"The family that owns the café named it after their father and husband who went missing when Guernica was bombed. They will be here any minute," said the woman.

Asier thought long and hard. He had been told by a neighbour that his family was dead. I saw my town being bombed. So many crazy thoughts passed through my head just at that moment. I am with Ashlin now. Were my son and my daughter alive too?

"What's wrong?" Ashlin asked. My body went into shock and I ran into the café for a large whiskey. I eventually explained my dilemma to her. Now, Ashlin is the very accommodating type and immediately came up with a suggestion.

"Why don't we all arrange to meet up somewhere and discuss what's happened to everyone over the past forty years?"

I was wary of this suggestion. How could I face the mother of my children after all these years? I was in love with Ashlin but once loved Naiara. What should I do?

I saw a group of people approach the café and ran towards them. An older woman said, "You look like my husband, Asier."

I stood up, blessed myself and cried, "I am Asier."

Naiara fainted.

Ashlin got her some water and we all went to sit in the café.

It was so moving to be reunited with my son, Aitor, and ultimately, my daughter, Agurtzane, after such a long time. And I even had grandchildren!

The café was next to the church. Without a second thought, Aitor went into the bell tower and started ringing the bells like a man possessed.

This time, no German and Italian planes flew by and scores of people made their way to the café.

"My father, Doctor Asier, has returned from the war," shouted Aitor.

I listened intently as to what everyone had been up to. *Jesus*, I had missed so much.

Naiara was in shock. When she came together, she arranged a dinner for family and old friends in the café. I listened intently as to what everyone had been up to. *Jesus*, I had missed so much.

"How did we miss each other after the bombing?" I asked Naiara.

"It was chaos. There were government soldiers everywhere. I stayed with my sisters for five days before returning home," said Naiara.

It was at this point I told my family and friends about killing an Italian soldier and how I couldn't return to the Basque region until Franco was dead.

I spent the following weeks telling everyone about my time in Scotstoun. I assured them that my stepson was making plans to catalogue our lives in the form of a book and I would try to get a Spanish edition printed.

Before coming to Spain, I promised to show Ashlin the parts of Spain I loved. When I arrived, I didn't want to leave Guernica and my family and friends. We, therefore, put our travels off for a month.

Asier and Ashlin tour Spain

The Americans I have met often explain to me how they have 'done' Europe during one single vacation. If they spend more than a day in Spain, they have a desperate sense of having failed to make any significant progress. It's not going to be one of those journeys from point A to point B. Though that might look to be the quickest way, as the crow flies, it misses out on all those random chance meetings that you have when you meander, like the river. Like the time I sat down for a coffee with an old couple to discuss historical events. I do not recall their names, but their take on the past was quite an eye-opener for me.

I had nothing but unanswered questions, whilst, for them, questions no longer mattered: events had happened in their lives, some of them very traumatic, but somehow they had reached an accommodation with the past.

"Life deals you a hand of cards," said the old man, "and you, in turn, deal with whatever you're given. Even during the Civil War, life carried on in a manner as close to normal as circumstances would allow. We didn't stop having babies, just because there was a war going on." I asked him about his experiences during the war, without enquiring which side he fought for. After all, after nearly forty years, surely we should all be prepared to bury the hatchet, and not revert to our tribal allegiances?

"When you reach my age," he continued, "and have the luxury of living off a small pension, you no longer have to satisfy a boss or some other authority figure. It's a huge feeling of liberation. You're almost back to that sense of disinhibition you had as an adolescent, before you had to work for your living, which consequentially meant working for your master, who had a hold over you until you had paid off all your indebtedness to the world."

Was this an opportunity for me to seek some advice to resolve my dilemma, perhaps? Could this man, or his wife, for that matter, help me get to the truth about what events had happened since 1937 that impinged on my life? I asked the couple how I should proceed in my quest for the ultimate truth. The old lady gave me some wise words of advice, prompting me to re-examine my whole understanding of the concept of truth. "Whose truth are you seeking?" She asked. "You do realise that there are multiple versions of the truth, don't you?"

I kind of understood her point, imagining that, after the Spanish Civil War, the victorious side would come to write a totally different account of events to that of those that were on the losing side, and so I put this point to her. "Two different histories, *deux Glasgow*," she remarked. My knowledge of French reminded me that this word is the French for story, as well as for history. I was being encouraged to understand that the reason why truth is such a fragmented concept is that no two people see the world in the same way. So, now I thought I really did understand: Ashlin and Naiara would have slightly different recollections of the same events that I had experienced.

"You're gradually getting there," interrupted the old man, "but there's one more realisation you have yet to make." I was confused. Whatever was he alluding to? "Your own story," said the old man, "it changes over time. You probably won't have noticed, but that's how we learn to live with ourselves. A little elaboration and embroidery, here and there. What began as an angry response to events will mellow as time goes by, as forgiveness begins to put a slightly different complexion onto past events. You will have unconsciously rewritten the script of your own personal story. Truth is really fiction, oh, and vice-versa, by the way!"

This revelation gave me quite a lot to think about. I almost had the impression I was writing a novel, a work of fiction, with myself as the protagonist and Ashlin, John and Naiara seemingly offering a whole plethora of alternative endings to my story. But life isn't like that: once the choice is made, you can't go back and say, "Oh, I didn't like the way that panned out, so I'll opt for a different outcome!" My dilemma—if the reader has not yet figured it out for himself or herself—is which relationship survives?

Basically, is it the one with Naiara and my, by now adult children, with children of their own, or is it with Ashlin? This isn't a story where everyone can live happily ever after; how credible would that be?

Procrastination seems the obvious answer, at least it does for me in my presently confused state of mind. I suppose you could call my peregrinations across Spain a kind of displacement activity. Indeed, I might even consider covering the same ground, again and again, in seemingly endless iterations, just to convince myself that I have returned to Spain after so many years in exile. I see the banners hanging from the windows, begging for Basque freedom fighters imprisoned many miles from their homes to be returned to face detention nearer to their loved ones. Separation is a punishment for those left behind.

I follow the *Camino* as before. There are shell symbols set into the pathways to mark out the route. I try to emphasise to Ashlin how important this visit is for me. It is a fantastic opportunity to spend so much time here in Spain, as well as in Euskadi. And yet, as we travel south by train towards Madrid, the landscape itself suddenly takes on a more menacing aspect: am I safe here in what has for me always seemed like hostile territory?

On our arrival in Madrid, I decided to take Ashlin to see the amazing art of Goya on display at the Prado Art Gallery. I observed her experience simultaneously fascination and revulsion as she saw the violence that he depicted. Since the last time I was here, the gallery has been extended in such a way as to impose some sense of order. The Spanish school is clearly delineated, though Italian, Dutch and British art is also on display elsewhere in the collection. So much for art: now it's time for Ashlin to get bored, as we visit the football grounds of Real Madrid and Atletico Madrid. Well, maybe not so boring after all?

I am delighted to be able to tell her that Atletico was founded with the help of three Basque players. Real was always the Establishment's team (royal), but Franco seems to have swapped his allegiances—at least as far as football was concerned—supporting first one side and then the other. The support undoubtedly wasn't mutual!

We move on in our epic journey to the ancient city of Cordoba, and promptly book a tour with the Spanish guide. I stress *Spanish* because she plays down the importance of the Moors and highlights the contribution the Spanish have made to the town's culture. She seems to find nothing bizarre about them having erected a Catholic church inside the existing mosque. It seems a strange idea to me. We travel on towards Seville. Ashlin remarks on the bright orange strip of the local football team.

I remind her that a lot of marmalade is manufactured here. Oranges are a very significant feature. We enter yet another art gallery. But this one has us spellbound for nearly four hours. I don't recall what the time was when we went in.

And finally, I have a treat lined up for Ashlin: It is a performance of Bizet's Carmen in the very city where that girl worked in a cigarette factory. Lots of flamenco dancing is how I recall the night. There might have also been some drinking! I am reminded how good music can be at lifting your spirits. We return to our hotel still singing those memorable songs.

The next day, we are standing on the corner of a street where everyone is eagerly awaiting the time when the *pasos* will be paraded through Seville, just as they have been in most towns across the length and breadth of Spain for centuries. And here comes one now! These ancient relics from medieval times: however do human beings manage to carry them on their heads? Hard to calculate how many men are under there; could be as many as forty, I don't know. Eventually, I see one man emerge with a cloth tied around his head. In some towns, they carry the *pasos* up steep hills to the local church, I am told.

Later, I am reminded of how easily symbols can be misinterpreted, or even hijacked for nefarious purposes. Visitors to Spain could be forgiven for thinking the Ku Klux Klan had arrived, but on closer inspection, we see that these are not the familiar white robes and hoods: in fact, we see young children donning these cone-shaped masks and walking along in a torchlight procession, each of them carrying a lighted taper. This all happens quite late at night, by which time you might have expected such young children to be in bed. But they love the experience!

And finally, as part of our journey through classical Spain, we head for Granada and the amazing vision that is the Alhambra. You have to admire the Moors' ability to harness the power of water. Ashlin loves the Fountain of the Lions. Then there's the brilliant architecture with those unmistakeably Islamic horseshoe arches. As in other religions, idolatry is a crime, but those amazing geometric shapes alongside Islamic calligraphy more than make up for the lack of images. I understand the famous artist, Maurits Escher, gained a lot of inspiration for his work through studying what are as many as seventeen possible variations of 'wallpaper' patterns in arriving at his intricate tessellations.

I alert Ashlin to the fact that even pop groups (and that includes Basque pop groups) were inspired by this place. And going from the ridiculous to the sublime, we hear that a recording of Andrés Segovia is about to be made right here.

And next, we travel up to Ronda. What a spectacular view! But don't look down just yet, I caution Ashlin. You need someone holding on to you, just in case you get the Peter Pan urge. 'Ask not for whom the bell tolls: it tolls for thee!' Thus, echoing John Donne's famous words, Hemingway chose this theme for one of his books about the Spanish Civil War. I decided not to tell Ashlin about the terrible fate that awaited those unfortunate souls who happened to find themselves on the wrong side at this point in history. Suffice it to say that their deaths involved a protracted descent from the cliffs.

But wait! We have omitted that part of Spain which has so much in common with Euskadi. We must head off now to Barcelona in the Catalan region which, like us, has been demanding independence from Spain for some time now. Mind you, the Catalans have not always been our friends: it's just that now, we have a perceived common enemy—Spain! Much like that unholy alliance forged between Churchill and Stalin against Hitler, in many respects, I reflect.

I must admire the inspirational work of Gaudi, the architect chiefly responsible for *Sagrada Familia* church. So unusual. More like the icing on the cake than the more traditional style of building Glasgow in Spain. Looking at other examples of Gaudi's work, I must wonder how they remain intact, seeming, as they do, to defy gravity in some cases. Admittedly, it is beautiful architecture—though some (including George Orwell) would disagree. I think Gaudi intended his buildings to mirror nature.

Traditional buildings are almost by definition diametrically opposed to any naturally occurring phenomenon, featuring straight lines, as opposed to Gaudi's preferred curves. His *Tree of Life* reminds me of our own Tree of Guernica, and looking all about me when I go inside Sagrada Familia, I see extensions of this arboreal theme. And yet, it was still a place of pilgrimage and worship, reminding me, in some ways, of the cathedral we had recently visited in Seville.

For some reason, I had in my mind that Sagrada Familia reflected similar ideas to those of Charles Rennie Macintosh whose work in Glasgow I had greatly admired. Another memory I have is of one of my visits to Edinburgh when I took in a trip to Rosslyn Chapel, which dates to the 15th century. For here, in Barcelona, within the Sagrada Familia, there were similar religious themes, both literal and symbolic: I particularly liked the plan to include a bull (Saint Luke), an angel (Saint Matthew), an eagle (Saint John), and a lion (Saint Mark) on 4 of the proposed 18 spires.

How sad that in 1926, Gaudi's life was tragically cut short by 'silent death', recalling the nickname of those trams back in Glasgow. Obviously, very few architects of grand projects such as these live to see the fruits of their designs, but in Gaudi's case, the building was only about a quarter of the way to completion when he died. The Spanish Civil War seriously delayed any further work, and the Catalans themselves caused a lot of damage to the building at the time. Even today, it is only about 50% complete, and I don't think it will be finished any time soon.

We stroll together down *Las Ramblas*, and I must urge Ashlin to beware of pickpockets here, though I do not wish to prejudge all gipsies. Better safe than sorry, however. Once again, I'm drawn to football, but Ashlin dissuades me from indulging my passion, and we finally head for the railway station to book tickets to Vitoria. But before we leave Catalonia, I must take Ashlin up a mountain. Not really a mountain, but quite a trek! Here we go—just a gentle climb at first, but you need the perseverance of a pilgrim to make the summit, and it is well worth the effort.

On the way up, we notice microscopically sized daffodils. That reminds me, I must show Ashlin the botanic gardens in Blanes one day. And now our ultimate destination comes into view. We enter the basilica and are drawn to the famous black-faced Madonna which attracts so many pilgrims. I prayed softly and decided that, under the circumstances, all I could do was to give my love and time when and where it was needed.

When we returned to Glasgow, Margaret Thatcher's campaign was growing in momentum (She was Prime Minister of the United Kingdom from 1979 to 1990 and the Leader of the Conservative Party from 1975 to 1990). I couldn't live under another right-wing leader and Ashlin knew it.

Ashlin

Asier wanted to return home. In fact, it is fair to say, he needed to go home. He had spent more than thirty years by my side in Scotstoun and now it was time to return to the Basque region. I suggested we move to San Sabastian and in no time, we bought a beautiful little house looking onto the sea. Asier's family and friends were only a short distance away and visited often.

John stayed in the big house in Scotstoun and took care of his son, Julio, until he started university. When Julio met Esti and things began to get serious, John joined us in San Sebastian. He liked it so much, he bought a little place of his own.

Part Two
Haizean Peace Haven Birth

James and Julio, 1994/5

More than five hundred people attended Scotstoun Health and Well-being Centre's Harvest Festival. The gathering on 3 September 1995 attracted over 40 different nationalities, coming together in harmony to celebrate the arrival of autumn.

As a new resident, I went along to meet my new neighbours and hopefully, make some new friends. It was a very colourful affair with brightly coloured ribbons tied to just about everything. There were cooking demonstrations and food tasters from all over the world. There was music, games, sports, face painting and dance displays. Though I had been suffering from mild depression from mil, I watched and marvelled at how happy the people were.

I am trying to stand up to the demons jabbing relentlessly in my head. My life is out of control. Now it is time to throw in the towel. I can't take any more. I see no reason in delaying the inevitable. I don't want to go on living. And furthermore, I have no reason to.

He looked visibly upset. "What do you mean?" The doctor said.

"My love has gone. All my plans. Everything. Gone," I replied.

"But your ability to explore other ways of loving and in time relight your spark could, in theory, be achieved," said the doctor.

"I suppose," I replied.

"Good. Come to my house for dinner tonight. There may be a way I can help you."

This was strange. A doctor inviting you to his home? I didn't even know the guy, yet he was going all out to help me. I was touched and accepted his invitation.

Doctor Julio lives on Victoria Park Drive North in a beautiful three-bedroomed house looking onto Victoria Park.

He is married to Esti and they have three young children. They also have a brown Labrador, called Charlie. I bought a nice Rioja and a juicy bone and walked to their house. Spanish cuisine is very colourful, healthy and varied. That night, I felt a little uneasy, but Esti soon put me at ease with a glass of red wine and a welcoming smile. The food was great. To be honest, I didn't know what I was eating but tried a bit of everything nonetheless.

"You have a beautiful home," I remarked.

"Yes, it was once the home of three local war heroes: my father, Asier Santamaria, my mother, Ashlin, and John Oswald. My father, Asier, was a doctor, my mother, Ashlin, was a nurse, and my uncle, John, a journalist. They all worked in our community flat on Dumbarton Road at different times and for different reasons. My parents are now retired. I moved onto a studio flat on the Kingsway estate," said Julio.

"Hang on a minute. You know John Oswald? He has been my journalistic role model for as long as I can remember. He is a friend of my parents and visits them every year in Millport. He convinced me to travel and go to university and even helped me gain a scholarship from the Oswald Trust."

"Yes, he's my uncle. And a bit of a legend in these parts. He even took part in high-level government operations during the war. We know John and Ashlin were connected to an ancient family that owned most of the land in these parts, but we don't know much about how the three of them all met or what they got up to together. Also, we found a mystery box in the flat full of war memorabilia. My family and I would like you to catalogue its contents and make sense of the findings."

"Wow. That may take some time," I replied.

"That's not all. We would like you to create an International Peace Haven as a living legacy to our ancestors," said Julio. "You will live in the flat with a bicycle, expenses and pocket money. Should you agree, you will be the first residential custodian. If it is a success, you will receive a good wage."

"Do I know you, Doctor?" I said.

"I don't think so," he replied.

"Do you know me?" I said.

"Enough to get your spark back, *hermano*," he replied.

"You know I can't really speak Spanish?" I said.

"*No Glasgow*," he replied.

I was desperate. I lived in a high-rise studio flat on my own. I was lonely and broke. My girlfriend had dumped me. Journalism was dying and I needed a job. I agreed there and then.

James

1995

I moved into a studio flat on the Kingsway estate and received a letter from my girlfriend telling me it was over. After four weeks of drinking and chain-smoking, I made an appointment with the local doctor.

He told me I needed a new focus and offered me a job running Haizean Peace Haven with a room thrown in. I accepted immediately.

My own flat was nearby and so it only took me about an hour to move in. The three-bedroomed flat was clean, somewhat rustic and homely. The furniture was simple but classy. There were lots of pictures and scented candles. Immediately, I got a very positive feeling; a true house of healing. That said, there was still a lot of work to be done before it would be ready to invite international students to stay.

Family members named the project 'Haizean', which is Basque for 'In the Wind'. The name has lots of connotations, the most obvious being the sound, smell and sight of the planes that came to bomb the little town of Guernica, Asier's home.

My first task was to gain charitable status. Once I had submitted all the paperwork, all I could do was wait and fix up the flat. Everything must be just right on these forms and so they boomeranged between myself and government offices until everything was just perfect.

The aims of the project are to promote peace and protest through all forms of art, create a better understanding of different cultures and economic groups, and to bring people together to share ideas and experiences.

The International Day of Peace (Peace Day) is observed around the world each year on 21 September. Established in 1981 by unanimous United Nations resolution 36/37, the General Assembly has declared this as a day devoted to 'commemorating and strengthening the ideals of peace both within and among all nations and peoples'.

From the text of the UN Resolution.

Furthering the Day's mission, the General Assembly augmented the original resolution in 2001, fixing the date on 21 September Peace Day provides a globally shared date for all humanity to commit to Peace above all differences and to contribute to building a Culture of Peace.

It is a small project run by a committee of family members, trustees and myself. In my short term as a residential custodian, I have had to learn on the job. In time, I hope to visit Peace Centres and museums dedicated to peace around the world.

It is hoped that the project will link up with research groups focusing on Cultural Intelligence: Cultural Intelligence, cultural quotient or CQ, is a term used in business, education, government and academic research. Cultural intelligence can be understood as the capability to relate and work effectively across cultures.

Haizean will also accept students from the ERASMUS programme—a programme named after the Dutch philosopher, Desiderius Erasmus of Rotterdam, known as an opponent of dogmatism, who lived and worked in many places in Europe to expand his knowledge and gain new insights, and who left his fortune to the University of Basel in Switzerland. At the same time, ERASMUS is an acronym meaning European Region Action Scheme for the Mobility of University Students.

So far, I have learned that the Spanish enjoy one of the best lifestyles (and quality of life) of any European country and, indeed, any country in the world: in Spain, work fits around social and family life, not vice-versa. The foundation of Spanish society is the family and community, and the Spanish are noted for their close family ties, their love of children and their care for the elderly (who are rarely abandoned in nursing homes). In short, the three most important things in their lives are family, food, and football. The job is diverse and never boring.

I also get a real sense of doing good and self-worth.

At first, I didn't have a clue about funding and funding sources. This is when I made my first contact with Scotstoun Health and Well-being Centre. Peter, Linda and Jassim have worked there for years. They mainly deal with refugees, asylum seekers, poverty and community-related issues. It is situated at the bottom of a tower block, one of six, about half a mile from Haizean.

The first thing that struck me about the Scotstoun Health and Well-being Centre is its 'Tardis'-like persona: it looks so small on the outside, but there's so much going on inside. And most of the activities are free.

What I like about the centre is:

1. The time they give users to heal and stay well: medical practitioners do not have this time.
2. The knowledge and experience of staff and members; someone always has an answer to your questions, or they know someone who has.

Health is a state of complete physical, mental and social well-being and not merely the absence of disease or infirmity.

World Health Authority

At Scotstoun Court Health and Well-being Centre, they also examine emotional and spiritual well-being and the environment. The centre interacts with many other different agencies, giving a holistic approach to health and well-being.

They also communicate and work with groups who are well-resourced to deliver talks. I also like the fact that they are a pro-active organisation: they don't preach, they do. There are only three full-time staff, yet they all take part in the activities. The project is situated in an area with high socio-economical and multi-cultural diversity. They gave me lots of information and some of their volunteers even helped fix up the flat in preparation for the arrival of the international students. Our relationship continues to go from strength to strength.

On 7 July 1996, Haizean finally received charitable status. This meant I could now advertise for students and apply for funding. Finding it difficult to focus on my own, I decided to bring in my first student straight away. 10 applicants became 3, then I settled on Selena, a young Spanish woman who was coming to Glasgow to do a Master's in English Language.

I hadn't given her much thought until her taxi drew up outside. Selena turned out to be a twenty-five-year-old, pretty, petite woman coming to stay with a fifty-year-old man and a scruffy dog. I showed her to her room, then we had a short talk. "We'll talk more tomorrow when you are rested," I said.

In the middle of the night, I heard Selena crying. At first, I thought I didn't have the skills to deal with this sort of thing, but then I remembered this is what a journalist does. He listens. There would be lots of different people coming to 'Haizean', each with their own agenda. It was not my job to fix people, but to facilitate learning through shared experiences, good and bad. It was my job to create an environment for that to happen. *Scraps* had a different approach. He just barged into her room and jumped into bed with her. They both fell fast asleep. Job done.

Next day, after breakfast, I explained what Haizean was all about.

I then told Selena about the mystery box and how I was struggling to open it without damaging its ornate design and contents. Within ten minutes, she found a secret compartment containing diaries and photos. A breakthrough at last. We came across lots of photos, letters, diaries, food menus, leaflets, and all sorts of bric-a-brac.

The paraphernalia in the box was as interesting as it was varied. In truth, there was enough information to fill five or six books. I would never have managed this on my own.

James and Julio

Selena

James and Selena, 2017

Students make the project. Haizean just provides an appropriate environment to help guests articulate their ideas and feelings. Haizean is privileged to share the ideas and experiences of worldwide students and travellers that would otherwise be left 'Blowing in the Wind'.

> How many times must a man look
> up before he can see the sky?
> Yes, 'n' how many ears must one man have
> before he can hear people cry?
> Yes, 'n' how many deaths will it take till he
> knows that too many people have died?
> The answer, my friend, is blowin' in the
> wind The answer is blowin' in the wind
>
> Bob Dylan

Arriving in Scotstoun, I intended to research my roots and move on. When I took on the Peace Centre job, I certainly was not at peace with myself. I had a broken heart, I did not have money, I was forever complaining and I was struggling to survive. Asier knew this and said, "This is what made you the perfect man for the job. Only you can change you. You need more life tools. Emotional intelligence can be learned. It is not rocket science," he added. Mastering others is strength. Mastering yourself is true power.

He was right, but I wondered where a Thistle supporter got so much wisdom. Working at the Peace Centre not only educated me, it saved me. The young people blew away past anxieties and fears, allowing me to love again. Following my break-up with my Australian girlfriend, I feared women. It was as if they were from another planet and one could kill me. Selena said I had a kryptonite complex. Just like Superman. All the students helped me and my dog, Scraps.

The second part of the book focuses on the Haizean Peace Centre.

I was not in touch with my emotions and feelings. My biological father, John, had it worse. In his day, few people talked about such things. So many things have happened over the past twenty years or so and I will be sad to move on.

I intend to work part-time so I can spend more time with my family in Millport: yes, you guessed it, I married Fabiana (the island girl from Maderia) and we have two children. That said, I don't think Fabiana likes Scottish winters and we may split our time between Madeira and Millport or Spain (I have stopped planning too far in advance. I'll do what Fabiana thinks best).

Selena, my first student, has returned to Glasgow with her husband and two children. The children are at school, so she will be coming back to work at the Peace Centre. Selena gave me a wry smile when I told her I had a new box for her. "You have a lot of things to catalogue our database, library, thingy," I said.

"This is déjà vu," she said.

"The thing is, Selena, you are from the digital age and we now have lots of digital work. We will need a website, an email address, a blog, and a way to store students' art, etc. This will be an ongoing process, to infinity and beyond," I said, quoting from the toy, Buzz Lightyear.

"You're right, James. The days of storing information in giant boxes have gone. However, the more time we spend interconnected via a myriad of devices, the less time we have left to develop true friendships in the real world," she replied. Selena has a knack for saying the right thing at the right time; she's right, of course.

"I agree. I will work part-time on the project and ease my way out. We will bring in a resident custodian to help you. And I'm only a phone call away. And I will pop in when I visit Julio," I said.

"I will do my best," said Selena.

"Thank you," I replied.

"*De nada*," she added (you're welcome).

2023 marks the 85th anniversary of the bombing of Guernica and the 27th anniversary of Haizean.

Student Testimonials

Marcel Proust, the French novelist, observed that "the real voyage of discovery consists not in seeing new lands but in seeing with new eyes." He realised that by working with other people we learn about their cultures and become able to explore new ideas and prospects. Options that would not have occurred to us before stand out as obvious if we understood how other people experience the world.

People visit Haizean at different times and for different reasons. The students are the most important part of the project and every effort is made to make their stay as comfortable as possible. Any income generated by Haizean comes through residential stays, student ideas, observations and research.

Haizean also promotes:

- mindfulness and self-awareness
- emotional intelligence and resilience
- empathy, kindness and social responsibility
- harmonious and caring relationships
- a greater sense of well-being and purpose

In my time here, I have only had to ask a few people to leave. Today, we ask people what they will bring to the project and what they hope to get out of it along with two references. We also insist that they produce an artistic testimony before they leave. Here, in their own words, are just a few of them:

CHEN (Meaning Morning), Chengdu, China.

Chen was a bit dazed when she arrived in Scotstoun. She was thirty-one years old, petite and very polite. I wasn't sure if she would stay, but she did and educated us on Eastern culture. The two of us would talk about writing and how crazy and addictive it can become at times. Here is what she had to say:

When I arrived in Scotland, I took the name Susan. I come from Chengdu which is the capital of southwestern China's Sichuan province. Chengdu's history dates to at least the 4th century B.C., when it served as capital for the Shu Kingdom. Artefacts from that dynasty are the focus of the Jinsha Site Museum. The city is also home to the famous Chengdu Research Base of Giant Panda Breeding, a conservation centre where visitors can view endangered giant pandas in a natural habitat.

It was my intention to complete the creative writing master's course at Glasgow University. Before doing so, I applied and was accepted as a student at Haizean Peace Haven.

It took me a while to settle in. In the Scotstoun area, I would get a lot of strange looks from people. Other than Chinese takeaways, there didn't seem to be any Chinese people living here. This was not the case in nearby Partick, where a lot of Chinese students were living and attending university. Staying at the Peace Haven helped me examine Western values and traditions and talk about Eastern values and traditions. I also got the opportunity to volunteer at the Scotstoun Health and Well-being Centre.

After my first week at the centre, I thought to myself, I have never seen so many misfits before in my whole life. This changed over time. People attended the centre looking for hope. And to be healed. Some were beyond saving, but this did not stop the staff and volunteers from trying.

My favourite parts of the project were the garden, the walks and the women's group. I was made to feel welcome and felt very comfortable attending the centre. I was puzzled as to why they didn't have any Eastern therapies like yoga, meditation, massage, stress management, or mental health self-management courses.

There was a lot of apathy on the Kingsway estate and it seemed to me it needed a massive injection of hope and guidance. A health and well-being centre would surely benefit from someone who knew about health issues, e.g., a nurse. The Scotstoun Health and Well-being Centre was a good start, but they needed more staff, bigger premises and some young staff to take the project to the next level, for generations to come. Getting to travel around Scotland was a real treat: my family and friends were so envious of all the photos I sent home.

There were five more flats in the same building as the Peace Centre. I wanted to get to know the neighbours, so I asked James if I could put my 'Act local, think global', policy into practice. He agreed and I made up a poster for a community close barbeque. It was a great success and we all brought different food and stayed outside until midnight eating, drinking, listening to music and talking. A few of the neighbours remembered the Peace Centre when it was a doctor's surgery. Some even remembered Dr Asier and Ashlin and stories of the good deeds they performed during the war.

After that, I was accepted as Susan and not a foreign alien. (N.B. James: The yearly summer barbeque continues to this day and is now in its 8th year).

I would later find out that the first Chinese student to study at the University of Glasgow arrived in 1886 and there are over 1,500 students from China studying at Glasgow at present.

The city of Glasgow is a thriving contemporary city. Chinese culture is very influential in Glasgow, with a wealth of Chinese restaurants, supermarkets and traditional Chinese medicine stores in the city. The University of Glasgow established the Confucius Institute in association with Nankai University. It builds on long-standing research collaborations between the two universities and is strongly founded on research on China across the University of Glasgow in the social sciences, arts, and business, in particular through the Scottish Centre for Chinese Social Science Research.

When my time was up, James helped me find a flat-share in Partick close to Glasgow University. Every now and then, I pop in Haizean and the Health Centre for a coffee and I am always made to feel most welcome. This is a great project and a fitting legacy for three war heroes who were so anti-war.

Val, Sofia, Bulgaria

Val came from a Soviet-style housing project in Sofia, Bulgaria. He was a very serious young twenty-five-year-old man who was determined to improve his circumstances. His work ethic was superb and I immediately thought about taking him on as a long-term resident. Here is what he wrote:

On a warm June day, the year of 2004, I was sitting with my then 'best' friend in the cinema on *Große Straße 38*. We were about to watch the *Prisoner of Azkaban*. This was the third movie in the series and by that time was highly popular among the youth. I did not see nor read any of the movies or books because I did not meet many people. I did not have any idea who made the movie (or wrote the book). I thought it was a Hollywood production. It was my best friend's (only friend) wish to go and see it.

In fact, I did not go to the cinema much either, so I was very excited. Sitting on the soft brand new ergonomic chair, I was noting every detail in my surroundings—the little lights that shone on the path, the black patterned design wall, the cheerful quiet banter, and the collective expectation for the beginning of the movie. I did not know what to expect but I just relaxed and let myself go with the stream. At this point, I must also point out that for the last ten years, I have not left my apartment much.

The movie began and reality stopped. All I felt was time and space skipping on the background of existence and the magical world of Harry Potter was all there was. The old castles. The way of speech. The way they were dressed. And the nature. The nature was absolutely stunning! I had not seen such a wonderful land in all my life. Well, I did see magnificent landscapes across my country, but

116

this was a different kind of beauty. I remember sitting there, in the moment of coming back to reality and asking myself: *Where is this place? I so badly want to go there!*

I couldn't get Scotland out of my mind and applied to the Peace Heaven to get a taste of this wonderful land. Back then, I did not know exactly what it was all about. I expected the usual communal living where you see and talk to your neighbour occasionally. But when I moved in, I saw James on a regular basis. We talked for long periods. The conversation started from something ordinary and then the flow took it in all sorts of different directions. Whether the WWII or the current Labour policies or even the dress code in Japan.

I was really delighted that James took me out on car runs as this helped me build a better picture of the Scottish culture. If I had been on my own, it would have taken me twice the time. Interestingly, he did not show me the city but rather the natural wonders of Scotland. We travelled from the shores of Loch Lomond to the Western Isles. From all the little towns along the Clyde to the city limits of Edinburgh.

He left me to explore the city on my own. The first territory I explored was the West End. I am situated in Scotstoun which is really close to the West End. During my first days, I liked to wait for the sun to set, play an audiobook (usually *Slaughter House Five*) and walk to Partick. On my way, I looked at the beautiful solid buildings. The further I went, the more their colours changed from red to yellowish. Shops sprung up. And, upon reaching West End's limits, the city came to life with the streets full of people going to the numerous shops.

During the day on the main Partick Street, you could see a big towering building. I felt like in the game *Half-life 2*, where your mission is to reach the highest building. I later learned that this is the old university building. I really liked walking there. If it were not for the cars, you would feel like you were visiting distant times. I saw why the West End is such a sought-after place. It wasn't just because of the beautiful buildings, it was because the people who lived there charged the city with life.

One thing I noticed was the impatience of people. What would happen at bus stops is a person will check when the next bus arrives and if it is more than a quarter of an hour, then they will strike up a conversation with the closest person on the bus shelter. They will start joking about the timeless inaccuracy of the buses and will continue as if they have known each other for a long time. Until the bus comes that is. This happens everywhere in the world but, the occurrence of this event is very high in Glasgow.

However, one time I found myself at a bus stop with another guy who had just started up a conversation with me but, after a few sentences exchanged when he realised I was a foreigner, he did not keep the conversation for long.

Another thing is the presence of different cultures living together in peace. It was hard to assimilate as where I come from different ethnicities don't like each other much. However, the reality in Glasgow is such that everyone compromises for the short back of the other. For example, every time I board the bus, there are numerous languages spoken at once which sounds strange but people bear it. I think this is a very valuable lesson for a modern city. However, most foreign nationals aren't very confident. They always give way to you and apologise if you come in physical contact.

Another thing that made an impression on me was that everything is named after the street where they are situated and, by everything I mean companies, schools or day centres. There are plenty of examples across the city.

A lot of my new friends expressed their dissatisfaction with the way things were being done. For example, the architecture at times resembled a scary and inhospitable piece of grey matter. The way people spoke was unintelligible. And, there were so many rules to follow. But my deliberation allowed me to appreciate them for their true beauty. The ugly buildings did not seem as such anymore, in fact, they were part of the whole. In this place of the world, the way people spoke reflected their identity. And the rules are an irreplaceable part of a modern governing system.

Although, there are many things that separate us culturally, I have come to realise that as humans we are not that different. We all go through the same development. We all encounter the same family problems. And we all laugh and cry for the same reasons anyone would do.

Throughout my time on the project and in Glasgow, I also discovered a thing or two about myself. For example, I found that being nice to people of all ages and regardless of class or health does make a difference and actually pays off spiritually. When I was growing up, I thought it was really *uncool* to hang out with old folks. But I changed my appreciation when I volunteered at Scotstoun Health and Well-being Centre where I met and spoke to many old gentlemen and women.

Actually, they turned out to be the best people. Some of them were talking about the war and how hard it was to live back then. Others were talking about the benefits of being young and we should use it whilst we can. Sadly, society nowadays doesn't value old people much.

I think the project was more than successful for me as I managed to mingle better with the local culture. I enjoyed the outings. In five years' time, I see myself as a graduate student. Still working part-time to save some money. I will be looking to get a work placement and set off my career. Haizean Peace Haven has set me on that path.

Selena, Barcelona, Spain

The youngest person to visit Haizean was a twenty-five-year-old, Selena Sanchez, from Barcelona. Selena was in Glasgow to do a Master's in Creative Writing. Her first degree was in Communication Studies, but her true passions were writing, drawing, animals and singing. Coming from a poor background, it was important for her to find affordable, secure accommodation and make new friends. Here is her testimony:

Visiting Glasgow was my first time abroad and I remember crying a lot in my first weeks. My main problem was understanding Glaswegians and the language they were speaking. Then there was the weather: it rained all the time and the whole place looked dark and dismal. The surrounding environment was not what I was used to. I was all alone and just wanted to run away. I'm so glad I didn't.

James, the co-ordinator, lived at Haizean with Scraps, the dog.

In those early days, Scraps was my saviour. We bonded immediately and went on lots of long walks. When I returned to Haizean each day, Scraps would be waiting for me. He gave me something to look forward to and was such a good friend. My mum says, 'Sometimes we need someone simply to be there. Not to fix anything or do anything. But just to let us feel we are supported and cared about'. Scraps was my 'someone'.

My room was lovely, as was the flat. A cleaner called Senga came in once a week. I couldn't understand her at first. She took care of all my laundry and filled me in with all the local gossip. James said she was like a mother and not to get on her bad side. Allegedly, she would hide (tidy) all of James' things. One time, she 'planked' his teeth and he went nuts. I liked her a lot.

James looked after me and persuaded me to talk with my family daily. When I got my schedule from university, James explained about working in the health and well-being centre, house rules, and babysitting opportunities with a local doctor (to be honest, I only did this once or twice). He also told me that he would be taking me to see Loch Lomond, the Highlands, a few islands, Edinburgh, and Stirling. Most of my time was spent working at the Scotstoun Health and Well-being Centre, in Haizean and at the university.

Haizean and the health and well-being centre both had a real, warm, feel-good factor about them; you just knew you were part of something special. I attended the lunch club in the health and well-being centre and introduced the Women's Group to Catalan cuisine. I also got my first taste of Scottish cuisine which included porridge, square sausage in rolls, and chips with just about everything.

The Woman's Group on a Friday night was fascinating. There were more than 50 nationalities with at least 5 represented on a regular basis, uniting as one for a few hours for a 'brew, a bite and a blether', as they put it.

Then James introduced me to his twenty-one-year-old cousin, Jemma, who was also at Glasgow University. She showed me around and we hung out between classes. One day, she asked me to come to her house for dinner. Her house was close to Dr Julio's place, near Victoria Park. It was on this occasion, I met Jemma's brother, Martin or, as James calls him, Gonzo: the muppet with the big nose (I love the 'Glasgow' sense of humour).

Martin had just qualified as a lawyer and had a joint honours in Spanish. He lived in Valencia for a year and his Spanish was great. They both took me on lots of days and nights out. Edinburgh was the first place Martin took me on his own. I loved it. It was clean, arty, historically interesting, European, and chic, with lots of things to see and do and places to just sit and be. The people didn't seem as friendly as Glaswegians, but the city was beautiful.

Then he took me for a day that I will remember for as long as I live. Starting at Drymen, a little Scottish village, we made our way to a magical little project called *Tir na Nog*: land of the eternal youth. There were teepees, fairy walks, a gift shop and a café. Next, we made our way to Stirling Castle, the Wallace Monument and Rob Roy's grave. Then we headed further into the countryside to a little village called Killin. The picturesque little village was divided by an old bridge with streams of waterfalls running through it. We stopped to marvel at the glorious surroundings, enhanced by the smell of burning peat.

On the way home, we stopped at Falloch Falls, a stunning waterfall, and the Drovers Inn (more than three hundred years old). It was here I got my first taste of 'haggis, neeps and tatties'. The last part of the day was driving down the banks of Loch Lomond with the window open, listening to music. When Martin dropped me at Haizean, he gave me a big hug.

We shared the same interests and Martin and Jemma both played musical instruments, the flute and the harp. Their parents invited me to a music festival in Ireland. It was here, after a few beers, Martin kissed me for the first time. When we returned to Scotland, we started dating.

I think that this was a relief for James; he trusted Martin implicitly and it meant he wouldn't feel awkward driving a young woman all over. He even broke the house rules of 'no overnight guests', letting Martin stay at the weekends, if all the work was done.

Martin then invited me to a family wedding. I had nothing to wear but Jemma soon sorted that out with one of her outfits. She even did my hair and make-up. I felt like a little princess. The wedding was fascinating. Jemma played the harp as the married couple entered the beautiful banqueting suite. It was held in the countryside in a posh riding school.

Most of the men wore kilts and the ladies wore posh frocks. It was a wonderful experience. We all sipped champagne and danced all night. And I got to meet Martin's extended family.

Victoria Park was a place I visited often with Martin, Jemma, and Scraps. It is a beautiful, historic park that I cherish. The only thing that would make it better would be a European-style café.

In Glasgow, I loved the fact that all the galleries and museums had free entry. I loved the warmth of the public, and I loved the 'patter', though it took me a few seconds longer to understand. What I hated was the heavy drinking and smoking culture, racism, sectarianism, a decadent environment that suppressed self-belief, and ignorance, including bus drivers who zoomed by when you were only centimetres from the bus stop and teenagers who smashed things up for no apparent reason.

In Spain, the hospitality industry is our bread and butter, so we know how to serve, how to treat people properly. People don't expect and don't get great service here: they are apathetic receivers of anything dished out to them. Yes, they may complain verbally, but they seldom complain in writing, thus the problem is never addressed. They even give the head of housing in the city a nearly £250,000pa wage package, yet they still have food banks for the poor.

The buzzword in Glasgow is 'regeneration'. Personally, I feel this is not enough. Regeneration is nothing more than physical development. Everyone must play a part in the process. Scotstoun and Glasgow must learn from past mistakes. What is needed is 'auto-generation' where communities and individuals take control and responsibility for their own destiny.

My Ideas

1. Posters for the Well-being Centre to be put in every doctor's surgery, dental surgery, chemist, library, newsagent, and community centre in the area.
2. Educate primary and secondary school children on mental, physical, emotional, spiritual and social health, giving them the tools to deal with the difficulties of daily life.
3. Purchase a respite flat on one of the Scottish islands for the Well-being Centre staff and members.
4. Introduce salmon and seafood farms on the Clyde and restore trees and greenery to an acceptable level throughout the city.
5. A wider choice of accommodation, location and colour of house where possible.
6. Monitor the exhaust fumes from cars and buses on the Dumbarton Road corridor.
7. Day trips outside of the city to let people see what they have on their doorstep.

8.   More places to relax and just be, mingle and talk: benches on streets and backyards.

9.   Support for those with no reason to get out of bed: a team to tackle loneliness.

10. Better communication between all health care providers and statutory authorities using modern-day technologies, e.g., apps.

Looking back, I was never alone. The friendships I have made at Haizean and the health and well-being centre are still as strong as ever.

In my time in Glasgow, I either slept with Scraps or Martin and I always had wise old James to talk to at the 10pm talks; he would encourage students to share their ideas and voice their concerns at these meetings. He would also get us to make him tea and toast. Hopefully, I will return one day. My time at Haizean went by very quickly and I loved it.

It's fair to say little Selena brought a lot to the project with her knowledge of new media and communication. She was always bright, positive and cheery. I would even go as far to say that little Selena sparkled.

Tony, Ontario, Canada

The oldest person to visit the haven was sixty-year-old, Tony Duggan from Canada. He had recently lost his wife: his children had flown the nest and he was keen to map his roots in nearby Drumchapel. Tony was a handyman and took great pleasure in freshening up the haven. He participated in the men's group in the Scotstoun Health and Well-being Centre and spent a lot of time in libraries researching and writing about his past. Here is his testimony:

In 1954, Gene Kelly starred in a movie called *Brigadoon,* where two American tourists stumble across a mysterious Scottish village that appears for only one day every hundred years. Tommy, Gene Kelly, falls in love with Fiona and must choose between modern-day America and the old ways of Brigadoon.

My experience of first love also happened in a magical time and place that was full of colour, innocence, and freedom.

The scene was set, purely by chance, two years before I was born. One day, my father read an article in a newspaper about housing bosses taking bribes for houses. At the time, he was living in the Townhead area of Glasgow with my mother and three sisters. The flat, a single end, had no toilet, no kitchen and only one room. The environment was filthy by today's standards and people struggled to get by on a day-to-day basis. He was so angry, he wrote a letter to the housing department that night. The following week, he was offered a house in Lillyburn Place, Drumchapel.

The house was in a quiet cul-de-sac, was in perfect condition, and had two bedrooms, a bathroom and a kitchen. The back windows looked onto a sea of green fields, a giant water tower and a farm. My mother was over the moon and they moved in just before Christmas 1963.

Things went from grim to great overnight: as a family, they had never lived in a house with its own bathroom, kitchen and room space. They soon settled into their new community and made lots of friends.

In those days, no one locked their doors and the word 'community' meant something. Most had come through hard times and all the neighbours went out of their way to help one another.

The '60s kept giving and giving, jobs were plentiful and tons of new opportunities and experiences opened to all. People began to take holidays abroad, buy cars, and tour further afield. Churches got in on the act by opening social halls and organising mystery bus runs all over Scotland. Young people expressed themselves through music and fashion. Flower power sprung its roots with bright colours, dance, long hairstyles, music, festivals, 'groovy' new words and much more. The Beatles, the Rolling Stones, and many others churned out thousands of vinyl records in a battle to be number one.

For the first time, every home had electricity. Cookers, fridges, washing machines, carpets, record players, and radios became *must-have* items in every home. Previously, unvoiced masses were grabbing the headlines as good triumphed over evil; the Civil Rights movement in America was gaining momentum, laying seeds for future change and 400,000 people gathered to take part in a 'hippy' music festival at Woodstock Farm, America. It was as if we were coming out of a deep depression and the planet was wearing a smile.

My father didn't know it but the second half of the decade was about to deliver even more. At 6.50pm on 10 January 1965, he was blessed by the arrival of a son. After work, he travelled to Redlands Hospital in the West End of Glasgow to be with his wife and new baby. Meanwhile, back at the ranch, my sisters waited with bated breath to get their first glimpse of their new baby brother. Said enthusiasm soon wore off and was replaced by constant complaining and complete indifference. Cries of 'Do I have to watch him', or 'It's not my turn', were commonplace.

One sister took me out for a walk with her friend in my pram and forgot to bring me home. At the tender age of four months, she had left me outside Mills newsagent. Luckily, I was still there when she returned. Another sister let go of my pram on a hill and it was only by sheer chance a bus didn't hit me as my pram whizzed across a busy road.

When I was old enough to walk, things got better. Each morning, I would wake up before everyone else and would sneak into my mother's bed. She knew I was coming, as mothers do, and would just pull up the blankets without opening her eyes. In her arms, I was warm, secure and loved, and she gave me the nickname 'Snookums'; brilliant! On reflection, she let me away with murder. If she thought I needed sorting out, she would delegate the task to sister number two, Kathleen, the tomboy.

Overall, the girls were alright, although they did favour sister number three, Evelyn, and spoiled her accordingly. As it turns out, there were two other girls in our close who were the same age as me. Life was simple and I didn't have a care in the world; every day was play day.

The seasons were in tune with nature and the summers arrived bang on time. On our many adventures, we would jump, fish and fall in the nearby burn which had a haunted tree hanging over it called 'The Hairy Mary'. There were many horror stories surrounding this tree so we avoided it at all costs. We spent many hours chasing each other through the rolling fields that seemed to go on forever. There was sandpit in the vicinity that attracted children from other places, and the older boys made sure that they didn't step out of line. Cows came right into our backyard and my mother, who was not Indian, told me it was a sin to hit them.

The farmer kept horses in a special field and you were not allowed to play with them in case they bit or kicked you. Sometimes they wandered up to a wall and you could feed them. They sensed fear so you had to relax in their presence and let them do as they pleased. On one such occasion, I watched in awe as a big stud horse pissed in the breeze with his dangling fury in full view.

Sister number one, Marie, would track me down when it was time to come in. Embarrassed, she would chase me all over the street while the other children shouted and cheered. When tomboy sister number two, Kathleen, turned up, I would give up.

On Thursday, 25 May 1967, my father's favourite football team, Celtic F.C., won the European Cup. They were the first British club to lift the trophy and all the players hailed from in and around Glasgow. Ripples of this famous victory spread far and wide and it is still talked about today.

Next, televisions and telephones arrived in our homes. The world was becoming a smaller place and it seemed anything was possible. The next logical thing to do it seemed was to visit the moon. And so on 20 July 1969, Americans Neil Armstrong and Buzz Aldrin took one small step for mankind. This was watched by millions who gathered around TVs all over the world.

I'm still not sure why man visited the moon. Personally, I would have saved all that time, money and energy for a rainy day, or focussed on a cure for cancer. That's the problem with good times, after a while people think they will last forever and always want more. Just as change had entered my family's life overnight, the same would happen to me.

The writing was on the wall when I was sent to nursery school: being locked up from 9am to 3pm didn't sit well with my emancipated disposition. Then when I thought things couldn't get any worse, they sent me to a place called 'school' wearing a uniform and a balaclava. I had no idea I would have to go to this place every day for the next twelve years or so. School was no place for a guy like me.

On my first day, I punched a boy's nose when the teacher was out of the classroom and there was blood everywhere. The teacher returned to find me cleaning up the crime scene with the sleeve of my blazer. She went mental. Everything was falling apart. The family decided to move to a bigger house far away from all of my friends and my countryside paradise. The clock struck 12.01am, 31 December 1969, and the '60s were over.

We moved to a three-bedroom flat in Drumry Road, Drumchapel close to the border of Clydebank. Situated on a busy main road, I had no friends and nowhere to play. Two years later, I would come face to face with the unexpected death of my mother. I was only seven years of age and longed for my mother's warm embrace and times gone by. The only thing I could do was pray and stay away from my father who had turned to heavy drinking to dull his pain. In those days, there was no real help for anyone suffering a bereavement. My mother's death left a great hole in our family. It was a terrifying setting for any kid, to be literally left alone in the dark for long periods of time.

Given all the facts, I now realise why my father went to pieces. Today, the girls are all doing well and have produced their own 'new age' families with all that entails. I have wandered down a million dead-end streets in search of those simple, carefree days that in reality will never return. Nothing had come close to that magical decade, then as Gene Kelly did, I found a way to travel in time and place. All I have to do is close my eyes and listen to music and I am immediately transported to the place I heard it first. Simple! My paradise in Lillyburn Place no longer exists. Lost in time but forever in my heart.

Tony was great fun to be around. We still keep in touch over Skype. He has a new wife and I hope he brings her to visit Scotland one day.

Takehiro, Hiroshima, Japan

Takehiro Hamamoto, or Hama, was a forty-five-year-old sushi chef who had come to work in Glasgow. He had been working in London for ten years, so I assumed his speaking, listening, reading, and writing skills would be good. Not so.

I met him in a café/bar and told him all about Haizean Peace Haven. The very next day, he turned up at the door. Out of pure curiosity, I interviewed him on the spot. His command of English was limited at best. And his listening skills were even worse. As I had never met a Japanese person, I asked him to join our little community.

Chen helped Hama put the following testimony together.

Hama was passionate about cooking (His cooking skills were beyond reproach) surfing, swimming, ballroom dancing, and travelling. Each night, he would tell stories about Japanese cities and culture. On his days off, he attended the health and well-being centre, again answering questions about Japan and introducing Japanese cuisine to the lunch club.

He was brought up in a seaside town close to Hiroshima, Japan. His mother told him stories about the war and how she remembers seeing a giant flash when the atomic bomb was dropped.

It is hard to say just what Hama got out of the project. I think the main things were friendships and unconditional acceptance. His stay took in the Christmas and New Year Period. On Christmas Eve, I asked him if he would like to celebrate Christmas dinner at my sister's house. He agreed.

That night, around 1am, I heard lots of noise in the hallway. I got up only to see Hama standing there with his surfboard. "I go surfing. Pease Bay. Good waves," he said. By this time, I knew not to argue, even though it was minus 10 degrees Celsius and snowing. I gave him my sister's telephone number and asked him to be there by 3pm.

At 4pm, he called from the hospital. "I'm in hospital. Man with dog on cliff see me. Helicopter save me. Nearly dead."

"My god. Are you alright?" I said.

"Yes. No operation, just tea and toast."

This is what he told us about Japan during war times:

Kamikaze, 'divine wind' or 'spirit wind', were suicide attacks by military aviators from the Empire of Japan against Allied naval vessels in the closing stages of the Pacific campaign of World War II, designed to destroy warships more effectively than was possible with conventional attacks.

Kamikaze aircraft were essentially pilot-guided explosive missiles, purpose-built or converted from conventional aircraft. Pilots would attempt to crash their aircraft into enemy ships in what was called a 'body attack' in planes laden with some combination of explosives, bombs, torpedoes and full fuel tanks—accuracy was much better than a conventional attack, the payload and explosion larger. The goal of crippling or destroying large numbers of Allied ships, particularly aircraft carriers, was considered by the Empire of Japan to be a just reason for sacrificing pilots and aircraft. These attacks, which began in October 1944, followed several critical military defeats for the Japanese.

Whilst the term *kamikaze* usually refers to the aerial strikes, it has also been applied to various other suicide attacks. The Japanese military also used or made plans for non-aerial Japanese Special Attack Units, including those involving submarines, human torpedoes, speedboats and divers. The tradition of death instead of defeat, capture, and perceived shame was deeply entrenched in Japanese military culture. It was one of the primary traditions in the Samurai life and the *Bushido* code: loyalty and honour until death, as the Japanese perceived it.

In Japan, there is a word, *omote*, which refers to the public, formal, and conventional aspects of behaviour. This can refer to ingrained patterns of behaviour, such as how close to one another people stand, or who shakes whose hand first at a meeting. It also can allude to behaviour in business affairs and events in a business setting. *Ura*, which is more valued, refers to the private, informal, and unconventional aspects of culture.

Japanese people see this mode of behaviour as more valuable and meaningful, however, one only acts this way with close friends or family members. The Japanese value outside appearances very much. This is not to say that they do not value what is private and hidden, but much importance is placed on one's presentation and appearance.

To demonstrate this point, the Japanese businessman is compared to a Samurai warrior or kamikaze pilot in The Idea of Japan. The Japanese know that you never come to a negotiation showing your true nature.

Social ranking and status play a part in many major institutions that one goes through in a lifetime. In Japan, everyone is aware of everyone else's age. In some companies, newsletters that display the ages of employees are produced for internal distribution. Vertical ranking, based mainly on age, determines everything from the location of desks in a classroom to the order in which cups of tea are distributed. These rankings are even pervasive in the language, which has different ways of addressing others regarding their age, whether older or younger.

Traditionally, the Japanese place great importance on the concept of *wa*, or group harmony. The value of the common greater good is more important than valuing one's own needs. This principle is applied in schools, as well as social groups and, later in life, the workplace.

Hama was very polite and mannerly. He would take his shoes off before entering the Peace Haven and would call me James San. Hama looked very young and sometimes acted very childlike. He would take everything literally and you had to watch everything you said to him. At times, he was very demanding and you never entered the kitchen when he was preparing food.

He didn't want to leave the project and he still returns for a few nights every year. My neighbours and the people at the centre really like him. For me, he was a learning curve. He left with a better command of English and friends for life. Put simply, a headstrong, surfing sushi chef that takes a while to understand.

Slav, Moscow, Russian Federation

Slav is a thirty-four-year-old doctor of chemistry from Moscow. He was working with Glasgow University on an international project to produce healthy biscuits. Visiting Haizean was his first time out of Russia. He was a very proud young man and gave us all a deep insight into Russian politics and culture. Here is his testimony:

People in Scotstoun have different values from people back home. Ordinary people in my country are not as rich. Here they treat brands like Apple, as if they were religions. The quality of life seems to be a little better here, though I don't think I could let go of some of my deep-rooted principles. Culturally, people are a lot more mannerly here. James made sure that he took me on lots of days out, showing me many beautiful places. Whilst I was there, it was just James and me. He told me it was my job to cook and do the dishes, so he could sample Russian food. He also gave me a lot of his time, mainly listening. He was a very gentle man and a great communicator. Above all, he was fun.

We read poetry and listened to music. Then we discussed what they meant to us, if anything. I particularly liked this one:

Invictus

Out of the night that covers me,
Black as the Pit from pole to pole,
I thank whatever gods may be
For my unconquerable soul.

In the fell clutch of circumstance
I have not winced nor cried aloud.
Under the bludgeoning's of chance
My head is bloody, but unbowed.

Beyond this place of wrath and tears
Looms but the Horror of the shade,
And yet the menace of the years
Finds, and shall find, me unafraid.

It matters not how strait the gate,
How charged with punishments the scroll,
I am the master of my fate:
I am the captain of my soul.
William Ernest Henley, 1849-1903 ·

This was the poem that gave Nelson Mandela strength when incarcerated on Robben Island. We discussed this at great length.

Slav at Robert Burns' Cottage

I then shared the song *Ignoreland* by the American band, R.E.M. The song's lyrical content is political, referring to the conditions of the United States during the Presidencies of Ronald Reagan and George H. W. Bush.

R.E.M.
Ignoreland

These bastards stole their power from the victims of the Us v.
Them years, wrecking all things virtuous and true.
The undermining social democratic downhill slide into abysmal Lost lamb off
the precipice into the trickle down runoff pool.

They hypnotised the summer, Nineteen seventy-nine.
Marched into the capital brooding duplicitous, wicked and able, media-ready,
Heartless, and labelled. Super US citizen, super achiever, mega ultra power
dosing. Relax.
Defence, defence, defence, defence. Yeah, yeah, yeah.
Yeah, yeah, yeah. Ignoreland. Yeah, yeah, yeah. Ignoreland. Yeah, yeah, yeah.

The information nation took their clues from all the sound-bite gluttons.
Nineteen eighty, eighty-four, eighty-eight, ninety-two too, too. How to be what
you can be, jump jam junking your energies.
How to walk in dignity with throw-up on your shoes

They amplified the autumn, nineteen seventy-nine. Calculate the
capital, up the republic my skinny ass. TV tells a million lies.
The papers terrified to report Anything that isn't handed on a
presidential spoon,
I'm just profoundly frustrated by all this. So, fuck you, man. (Fuck 'em)

Yeah, yeah, yeah. Ignoreland. Yeah, yeah, yeah. Ignoreland.
If they weren't there we would have created them. Maybe, it's true, But I'm
resentful all the same. Someone's got to take the blame.
I know that this is vitriol. No solution, spleen-venting, But I feel better having
screamed. Don't you?

They desecrated winter, nineteen seventy-nine.
Capital collateral. Brooding duplicitous, wicked and able, media-ready,
Heartless, and labelled. Super US citizen, super achiever, mega ultra power
dosing. Relax.
Defence, defence, defence, defence. Yeah, yeah, yeah.
Yeah, yeah, yeah. Ignoreland. Yeah, yeah, yeah. Ignoreland.
Yeah, yeah, yeah. Ignoreland. Yeah, yeah, yeah.

The song gives me hope in an era where protest songs are not so common.
Finally, I wanted to discuss 'Tank Man' (also known as the Unknown
Protester or Unknown Rebel). Tank Man is the nickname of an unidentified man
who stood in front of a column of tanks in June 1989, the morning after the
Chinese military had suppressed the Tiananmen Square protests of 1989 by
force.

This image went all over the world and shows that we can all stand up for peace. Haizean was a great experience and I have invited James to visit Moscow and sample my world.

To this day, I keep in touch with Slav and will definitely visit Moscow one day. James.

Michael, Heidelberg, Germany

Brought up on a farm near Heidelberg, Germany, Michael was a very sensitive and studious young man. It was obvious that he felt bad about the bombing of nearby Clydebank and about WWII and set about finding a way to reconcile these feelings. We went on many long walks and had lots of talks about reconciliation. He then introduced us to the Stalingrad Madonna.

The Stalingrad Madonna (German: *Stalingradmadonna*) is an image of the Virgin Mary drawn by a German soldier, Kurt Reuber, in 1942 in Stalingrad (now Volgograd), Russia, during the Battle of Stalingrad.

The original is displayed in the Kaiser Wilhelm Memorial Church, Berlin, whilst copies now hang in the cathedrals of Berlin, Coventry and Kazan Cathedral, Volgograd as a sign of the reconciliation between Germany and the United Kingdom and Russia, who were enemies during the Second World War.

The piece is a simple charcoal sketch, measuring three feet by four feet (900 mm × 1200 mm). Mary is depicted wrapped in a large shawl, holding the infant

Jesus close to her cheek. On the right border are the words *Licht, Leben, Liebe* (Light, Life, Love), from the Gospel of John. On the left, Reuber wrote *Weihnachten im Kessel 1942* (Christmas at the Siege 1942), and at the bottom, *Festung Stalingrad* (Fortress Stalingrad). *Kessel* (Cauldron) is the German term for an encircled military area, and Fortress Stalingrad was the label for the encircled army promoted in the Nazi press.

The picture was drawn by Lieutenant Kurt Reuber, a German staff physician and Protestant pastor, in December 1942 during the Battle of Stalingrad. Reuber wrote:

"I wondered for a long while what I should paint, and in the end, I decided on a Madonna, or mother and child. I have turned my hole in the frozen mud into a studio. The space is too small for me to be able to see the picture properly, so I climb onto a stool and look down at it from above, to get the perspective right. Everything is repeatedly knocked over, and my pencils vanish into the mud. There is nothing to lean my big picture of the Madonna against, except a sloping, homemade table past, which I can just manage to squeeze. There are no proper materials and I have used a Russian map for paper. But I wish I could tell you how absorbed I have been painting my Madonna, and how much it means to me.

"The picture looks like this: the mother's head and the child's lean toward each other, and a large cloak enfolds them both. It is intended to symbolise 'security' and 'mother love'. I remembered the words of St. John: light, life, and love. What more can I add? I wanted to suggest these three things in the homely and common vision of a mother with her child and the security that they represent." He added that he:

"…went to all the bunkers, brought my drawing to the men, and chatted with them. How they sat there! Like being in their dear homes with mother for the holiday."

Later, Reuber hung the drawing in his bunker for his unit celebration, which he described as a moment of Christian devotion shared by all the soldiers in his command.

When according to ancient custom, I opened the Christmas door, the slatted door of our bunker and the comrades went in, they stood as if entranced, devout and too moved to speak in front of the picture on the clay wall…The entire celebration took place under the influence of the picture, and they thoughtfully read the words: light, life, love. Whether commander or simple soldier, the Madonna was always an object of outward and inward contemplation.

The Madonna was flown out of Stalingrad by Dr Wilhelm Grosse, his battalion commander of the 16th Panzer division on the last transport plane to leave the encircled German 6th Army. Reuber was taken captive after the surrender of the 6th Army, and died in a Soviet prisoner of war camp in 1944. The Madonna and a number of letters from Reuber were delivered to his family. There they remained, until German federal president, Karl Carstens, encouraged Reuber's surviving children to donate the work to the Kaiser Wilhelm Memorial Church in Berlin.

Springer, Reuber's three children and Prince Louis Ferdinand (in his role as chair of the Memorial Church board of trustees) attended the dedication ceremony in August 1983.

The drawing and Reuber's letters were published shortly after the war, and Navy Chaplain Arno Pötzsch wrote an apologetic book of poetry entitled *The Madonna of Stalingrad* in 1946. The work became a powerful symbol of peace in the Cold War era, as well as part of the mythologising of Stalingrad and the events of the Second World War in German society. Copies were presented, and are displayed, in the cathedrals of Volgograd (formerly Stalingrad), Berlin, and Coventry as a symbol of reconciliation.

Similarly, a Cross of Nails from Coventry is displayed with the Madonna in the Kaiser Wilhelm Memorial Church.

Reuber painted a second similar picture in captivity around Christmas 1943. He was by this time in a prisoner of war camp in Yelabuga, some 1,000 kilometres northeast of Stalingrad, and the painting was made for the prisoners' newspaper. He titled it 'The Prisoners' Madonna'. Reuber did not live to see another Christmas, dying of illness a few weeks later, on 20 January 1944.

The Stalingrad Madonna has been on display in the Kaiser Wilhelm Memorial Church since 1983 and reminds churchgoers and visitors, young and old, of the horrors, the suffering, and the hatred of war. Today, Reuber's drawing functions as a stark symbol calling for peace in times of war.

It is also confirmation of the spirituality of a man who accepted his mission and lived his entire life in the service of his fellow human beings. The Biblical words, light, life and love, are like a bridge that can bring different people together in reconciliation—even in times of relative peace, which can never be taken for granted in Europe and beyond.

When Michael moved on, we acquired a copy of the Stalingrad Madonna from a church in Berlin and gifted it to Our Holy Redeemer's and Saint Margaret's churches, Clydebank.

Our Holy Redeemer's church has been there through the Clydebank rent strikes of the First World War, the General Strike of 1926, and the depression era of the early 1930s, and it narrowly survived being destroyed in the Clydebank Blitz in 1941.

Michael

Fabiana, Madeira, Portugal

Usually, we don't take short-term placements, but who could say no to such a touching letter:

Dear Sir,

My name is Fabiana, I am twenty-nine years old, and I work as a waitress in a hotel in Madeira. All my life, I have wanted to travel, but the wages we earn here don't allow this to happen.

I saw a programme on TV about your project and thought if I saved a little each month, I could perhaps come for a two-week visit when you are not so busy.

Your blogs are marvellous and I thought if I came to your project, I could experience lots of different cultures in one go.

This would be the only way someone like me could afford to do this.

Yours sincerely,
Fabiana

Fabiana, 2013

Well, she did come and I was determined to show her as much of Scotland as I could. Here is her testimony:

When I arrived at the project, James, Scraps (the dog), and a pretty young French woman called Avril, were waiting for me. James seemed awkward around me at first. He tried, much too hard to communicate and later told me he was threatened by my Latin looks. He couldn't relax and made no eye contact at all.

"It's my job in this project to support, inspire and electrify," he said. I just bust out laughing. He did too. "That was meant as a joke," said James. Following the 'Superman' style speech, things started to improve.

Avril was beautiful and knew everything about fashion.

All I knew about was cooking, food, service, and how to hard work for little pay. We had little in common but got on well, and would often take Scraps on walks to Victoria Park.

Victoria Park was great. It had a boating pond, lots of huge trees, a fossil grove, a maze, a children's area and many colourful plants. It was also where the Peace Tree was. James told me it was a healing park, where people would walk for hours letting the wind blow all their problems away.

At first, I was very shy and said very little at the ten o'clock debates. After a few days, I just chipped in when I could. Mainly, I just listened and learned from what was being said.

Here are the trips James took us on:

1. Glasgow to Drymen to Stirling Castle to Wallace Monument to Killin to Crainlarich to the Drovers (three-hundred-year-old bar), to Loch Lomond to Glasgow.
2. Glasgow to Inverary via the four lochs; Loch Lomond, Loch Long, Loch Goilhead and Loch Fyne.
3. Glasgow to Edinburgh and the Forth Rd Bridges.
4. Glasgow to Robert Burns' cottage.
5. Glasgow to Millport (we all cycled around the island and had lunch in a beautiful café).

The rest of the time was spent at the Scotstoun Health and Well-being Centre. Here I met people from more than forty different countries.

James said one night, "You can't fully see your life whilst you are in it. If you have a problem or want to see things in a different light, then stop everything. Go for a walk. Visit a park or a museum. Or better still, go on a holiday and reflect.

"You know, once I didn't come back from lunch. Impulsively, I booked a helicopter ride. The advert had been running all morning on the radio. And for thirty minutes, I floated above all my worries. Yet, one question stuck with me: what is it I do down there? Put a smile on others' faces and try, was my honest reply." Hmph. Quite a wise man, this James. I think I like him.

Before I left, James asked me out for a meal. We caught the bus and walked through the West End before coming to a Japanese restaurant. It was run by two sisters and was very oriental. James ordered for us both. Without question, it was the best meal I have ever had. He then took me to a *karaoke* bar. He sang three songs, looking at me all the while.

"Why did you pick those songs?" I asked.

"Two reasons," he said. "One it's how I feel about you. And two, they are the only songs I know right through," he added.

"But you haven't really spoken, or looked at me," I said.

"I have been watching. Your beauty scares me. And I didn't want to scare you," he said.

"Well, you didn't and I am going to make you hold my hand and listen to a Portuguese song as we walk home," I said. At that point, he gently kissed me on the lips.

Now I am back at work in Madeira, I have a new outlook. I figure, if I can't travel the world, then the world can come to me through work. I might even take up more languages. The two weeks went by very fast and I will keep in touch with everyone I met. And I would gladly recommend the project to other people.

Update: I'm now back in Scotland with James.

15 Haizean
Peace Centre 10 o'Clock

Debates

The café culture, across Europe, is an important part of people's everyday lives, and you can learn a lot about the locals and their traditions by simply exploring the cafés as you visit each country. You'll be amazed by just how much they differ from each other, and how much their traditions tell you about the people themselves.

So, every night, we hold a debate around 10pm in the lounge of Haizean, or what I like to call our very own Peace Café (HPC). Generally, the talks involve a hot drink, toasted cheese, cookies, and daily questions and answers.

Over the years, we have talked about many things including the Glasgow accent, NEDS (Non-educated Delinquents), health, free entry to museums, and eating and drinking habits.

Most European students can't understand why there are not more places to cross the road and why pedestrians are not king here. Some found the buildings dull and dirty and poor looking. Others found the warmth and friendly nature of Glaswegians made up for any small indiscretions.

All students came fully versed in curse words: I tried to teach them how to debate positively with regular English. And show them how more satisfying this was. The debates often threw up things I knew nothing of, e.g., when a Russian student stayed at the same time as a Japanese student. This was extreme. They seemed to hate each other and I didn't know why. Initially, I thought it was just a cultural thing: the Japanese are big on manners and etiquette, but the Russians are not.

After talking to both boys, I found out their countries had bad blood in the past. I pointed out that this was in the past and should they wish, it was time to move forward. They did and are still friends today.

Either I or a student would download or gather information for that night's talk. That person would either present the debate or lead a talk on a chosen subject. I have included a piece on Russia and the Spanish Civil War. I also encourage students to paint, draw, sing, write or produce any form of art that I can add to our library.

Russia and the Spanish Civil War

In the early 1930s, Joseph Stalin was deeply concerned about the spread of Fascism in Europe. To counteract the growing power of Adolf Hitler and Benito Mussolini, he encouraged the formation left-wing coalitions. This resulted in the Popular Front Government being formed in February 1936. This was followed by Popular Front Government in France in May 1936.

On 10 May 1936, the conservative Niceto Alcala Zamora was ousted as president of Spain and replaced by the left-wing Manuel Azaña. Soon afterwards, Spanish Army officers, including Emilio Mola, Francisco Franco, Juan Yague, Gonzalo Queipo de Llano, and José Sanjurjo, began plotting to overthrow the Popular Front Government. This resulted in the outbreak of the Spanish Civil War on 17 July 1936.

In July 1936, José Giral, the prime minister of the Popular Front Government in Spain, requested aid from France. The prime minister, Leon Blum, agreed to send aircraft and artillery. However, after coming under pressure from Stanley Baldwin and Anthony Eden in Britain, and more right-wing members of his own cabinet, he changed his mind.

Baldwin and Blum now called for all countries in Europe not to intervene in the Spanish Civil War. In September 1936, a Non-Intervention Agreement was drawn up and signed by 27 countries including Germany, Britain, France, the Soviet Union, and Italy.

Benito Mussolini continued to give aid to General Francisco Franco and his nationalist forces and during the first three months of the Non-Intervention Agreement sent 90 Italian aircraft and refitted the cruiser *Canaris*, the largest ship owned by the Nationalists.

On 28 November, the Italian government signed a secret treaty with the Spanish Nationalists. In return for military aid, the nationalist agreed to allow

Italy to establish bases in Spain if there was a war with France. Over the next three months, Mussolini sent to Spain 130 aircraft, 2,500 tons of bombs, 500 cannons, 700 mortars, 12,000 machine guns, 50 whippet tanks and 3,800 motor vehicles.

Adolf Hitler also continued to give aid to General Francisco Franco and his nationalist forces but attempted to disguise this by sending the men, planes, tanks, and munitions via Portugal. He also gave permission for the formation of the Condor Legion. The Legion, under the command of General Hugo Sperrle, was an autonomous unit responsible only to Franco.

Joseph Stalin now became concerned that the Nationalists would defeat the Republicans in Spain. He took the view that four extreme right-wing governments in Europe would pose a serious threat to the security of the Soviet Union. Although Stalin continued to support the idea of the Non-Intervention Agreement, he was now willing to supply the necessary military aid to stop a Fascist regime being established in Spain.

Stalin encouraged the Comintern to organise the formation of International Brigades. He also sent Alexander Orlov of the NKVD to advise the Popular Front Government. Orlov supervised a large-scale guerrilla operation behind nationalist lines. He later claimed that around 14,000 people had been trained for this work by 1938.

The Soviet Union provided considerable help to the Spanish Communist Party to improve its position in the Popular Front Government. This included the removal of the socialist Francisco Largo Caballero as prime minister and replacing him with the communist sympathiser, Juan Negrin.

Alexander Orlov also used NKVD agents to deal with left-wing opponents of the Communists in Republican-held areas. This included the arrest and execution of leaders of the Worker's Party (POUM), the National Confederation of Trabajo (CNT), and the Federación Anarquista Ibérica (FAI).

The Soviet Union were the main supplier of military aid to the Republican Army. This included 1,000 aircraft, 900 tanks, 1,500 artillery pieces, 300 armoured cars, 15,000 machine guns, 30,000 automatic firearms, 30,000 mortars, 500,000 riles, and 30,000 tons of ammunition.

10 Gemelos

James and Julio, 1998/99

"Over the years, I have learned a lot about Asier, Ashlin, and John's work from my patients. Their deeds and commitment to the community are still fondly remembered by the people of Scotstoun. Haizean is not just about the past. It's about right now and the future. I was lucky enough to have Asier and Ashlin as parents and Uncle John was never very far away either," said Julio.

"John gave me specific instructions. He felt it would be better for you to get to know our family before revealing who we were. He told me all about you when I was eighteen years old. He promised me that you would return one day," added Julio.

"I don't understand," I said.

"My life in Scotstoun was perfect. Too perfect in fact. I was glad to be known as Julio Santamaria. I didn't want to be in the spotlight. I didn't want to be an Oswald. John and Ashlin both understood. He left this letter for you," said Julio.

Dear James,

If you are reading this, then you and your brother have been reunited.

Yes, you and Julio (John) are brothers. There is no easy way to tell you this, but you are both my twin sons. I had you both with my girlfriend, Jackie White, who was much younger than me. She died shortly after giving birth to you both. I went to pieces and tried to numb my pain with whiskey.

Ashlin wanted to take care of both of you, but I knew she was busy planning the new surgery.

I, therefore, decided to place you both in a children's home until I got my head straight.

Father George Gillespie sent me to a place in Millport for rehabilitation.

I have never lost touch with you both, except during this time.

Whilst on the island, I became friendly with Lawrence and Lorraine O'Neill, who ran the post office.

They were desperate for a child. After a great deal of thought, I asked them to adopt you as long as I could visit and tell you everything on your eighteenth birthday.

They agreed.

Ashlin and Asier adopted your brother.

Your mother didn't want either of you to be tainted by sectarianism, so placing you both in the right homes was very important.

You looked the most like Jackie, so sometimes visiting was hard.

I told Julio on his eighteenth birthday. I almost told you at your eighteenth birthday party but was afraid I might stop you from travelling.

My whole estate has been left to you and I'm sorry if you see me as a coward. I've never stopped loving you boys and in truth, my family are my reason for living.

We will meet again soon. Love always,

John Oswald

11 My Return to Millport

James Millport, 2000

This was the first time I had been to the island for months. Mum and dad had sold the post office and were now running a small seafood café. I thought I would go for a beer and then surprise them. Who was I kidding? This is Millport. The grapevine extends all the way to the ferry boat and back.

As I entered the pub, my mum and dad were sitting at a table waiting for me. Both gave me the usual family hug. "So, son, should we head home now and have a big chat? Or just get drunk and do it tomorrow?" Dad said.

"I'm up for that. But I just want to say, I will never stop loving you both and you will always be my parents," I said. They both looked a little relieved and mum began to cry.

We talked everything through and they told me about a planned reunion of family and friends in Guernica. It was good to be home. I looked up some old friends and went fishing. So much had happened in a short period of time. Staying with mum and dad gave me breathing space to reflect. It also gave me time to go on long walks and cycle around the island.

Mum and dad lived in a four-bedroomed bungalow at Kames Bay, just before you come into the centre of Millport. We were finishing up one night in the seafood café, and mum said, "You know, this will be yours one day. Along with the house and our savings?"

"Lately, people have been giving me things I really don't feel I deserve. However, if you and dad intend to retire on the island, then I would gladly look after you. Besides, when I take a wife, we will need babysitters," I said.

She smiled and dad added, "It's a deal."

"Out of curiosity, what do you both think of the island of Madeira?" I asked.

"Where is it?" Mum said.

"Never mind," I said. I was still in touch with Fabiana and a thought occurred to me. If we were together, we could help mum and dad in the café and offer the spare room as a respite to Haizean, or even the Well-being Centre.

"So, you are my twin brother?" I said.

"Yes," said Julio.

"But my brother was called John?" I said.

"Yes, they changed it. It wasn't Spanish enough. And I just wanted to be me," said Julio. "I was brought up half-Spanish, but I can speak fluent Glaswegian when I have to," he added.

All I could do was cry. "Why did he leave his estate to me?" I said.

"I guess he knew Asier and Ashlin would take care of me," replied Julio.

"Couldn't you have told me all of this when I first met you?" I said.

"No, John wanted you to get to know us and to have the option to walk away from the Oswald label," replied Julio.

"But isn't he dead?" I cried.

"John Oswald is dead. Retired, so to speak. John Ritchie, our father, is very much alive," said Julio.

"What about Asier and Ashlin?" I said.

"Yes, the three of them live in San Sabastian," replied Julio.

"What the fuck? Are there any more secrets?" I said.

"Yes. Asier says expletives are the laziest form of expression," said Julio.

"And John?" I asked.

"He doesn't seem to give a fuck," replied Julio. We both smiled. "And the wife and family Asier thought he had lost in the Spanish Civil War turned up a while back," said Julio.

"Oh my god!" I said.

"Yes. Almost forty years later," said Julio.

"Anything else?" I said.

"Not really," replied Julio.

"What does that mean exactly?" I replied.

Julio just smiled and said, "Ah, yes. The man you saw on the night we parted as children was Asier. He's a Thistle fan. I support Partick Thistle too. I particularly enjoyed the 4-1 win over Celtic in the League Cup Final in 1971."

Evasive or what? "Is that right? Well, I support Celtic and I particularly enjoyed the 7-0 win over Partick Thistle in the league in 1973." We both embraced and laughed. I knew that this was the start of an interesting and loving journey. And so, the brotherhood was reunited.

For me, getting my wee brother (by two minutes) back has been the best part of this whole process. I have always felt there was some part of me missing.

Reunion

James and Family Guernica, 2001

My parents, Julio, Esti, and their children planned a visit to see John, Ashlin, and Asier in San Sebastian. I decided to go along too. We flew to Bilbao and took a bus to San Sabastian. I was so excited. Asier, Ashlin, and John were all at the bus station when we arrived.

We all embraced and piled into two Glasgow cars. "I'll take James, Lawrence, and Lorraine," said John. "I'll show them their rooms and we can all meet up this evening at your place," he said, looking at Ashlin and Asier.

"OK," replied Ashlin.

John had a three-bedroom bungalow on the edge of town. We unpacked, showered, and then had a drink in John's garden.

The garden smelled as good as it looked and I had no idea what most of the plants were. Ashlin and Asier lived about five minutes' walk away. It was a long hot summer's night and we made our way to the party.

By now, they were all in their eighties, though you would never have guessed. Asier was a tall handsome man. He was keen to hear all about my travels and listened intensely. He spoke in a soft, clear, compassionate voice. Ashlin was one of those ladies whose beauty did not reflect her age. Her eyes, her smile, her gentle manner; in fact everything about her was beautiful. She would always touch your hand or arm when you were talking to her. I liked that. Paradoxically, she was a strong woman who had been through so much.

My biological father, John, was a large man. He was a little fat, liked to sing, but above all was good fun. He smoked a pipe and was a good listener.

The party was in Asier and Ashlin's four-bedroom villa, overlooking the sea. Asier's Spanish family and friends were there too. Most of the time, I didn't know what was going on. Not speaking Spanish didn't help. When John and Asier brought out their guitars, the party really got going. I really enjoyed their rendition of *Viva la Quinta Brigada*. The Basque traditional dancing was a treat to watch. And the food was out of this world. I was wary that mum and dad would feel left out, so I made sure I sat at their table. Dad said, "Don't be afraid to mingle. There are a lot of beautiful women here."

Mum added, "Just make sure the woman you are kissing at the end of the night is not your cousin." We all laughed.

The next day, John took Julio and me for a long walk into the hills, looking down on Guernica. He said to both of us, "This is where it all kicked off."

"I guess you know the rest from our diaries," he added. John then took me aside for a chat.

"I hope you are not angry with me, son. When your mother died, I lost my mind. I was in no fit state to be a father. My only comfort in those dark days was the bottle. My friend, Father George Gillespie, sent me to a place in Millport to dry out. It was there I met your parents.

"When I returned to Scotstoun, I had a long talk with Asier and Ashlin. I then decided to let Ashlin and Asier adopt one boy and ask your parents if they would adopt you. They were delighted. The way I saw it, both couples were working and it wouldn't be fair to ask either to adopt you both. Jackie insisted she didn't want you to be tainted by sectarianism too. Being out of Glasgow, Millport was perfect.

"I promised both couples not to tell you who your biological parents were until your eighteenth birthday. I have tried not to keep you apart. The best I could do was to make sure the three of us spent as much time together as possible, and provide financial assistance. I'm not built for touchy-feely things like Ashlin," he said.

"I know how you feel. My twin, Julio, is emotionally stronger than me." We both smiled.

At the end of the night, I said, "Having read your diaries and researched your lives, I feel I know you. The process of putting the book together has been a long one. It has helped me learn more about myself and my roots. For this, I will be eternally grateful. I hope you are happy with the outcome. I am humbled and honoured to have taken on this task. To me, you are soldiers and my generation owes you our lives."

At this point, Asier stood up and asked, "Is there anything else you want to know?"

"Well, yes. I don't have any pictures or details on Ashlin, John and Jackie's wedding," I replied.

Ashlin added, "That's because we have them here. They are private and will be passed down to the family in time."

Meeting Asier, Ashlin, my biological father, John, and visiting the Peace Centre totally blew me away (The Gernika Peace Museum, formerly known as the Gernika Museum, opened on 7 April 1998). Collectively, they have fuelled my spirits and bolstered my soul.

PART TWO HAIZEANn't know why. The event was supposed to run from 1pm until 4pm, yet I was still talking to people well after 9pm. After the sun went down on proceedings, the harvest moon punched a hole in the midnight sky,

ushering in a period of hope and change for the residents of Scotstoun. The starlit starlight guided me home; new friends were found and no longer alone.

The next day, I went for a walk and stumbled across a piece of derelict land known locally as 'The Homie'. At first, I didn't recognise the place: there were too many distractions and noises that I wasn't familiar with; the buildings were different and the tram cars had been replaced by an army of buses and infantry of cars and lorries.

When I returned at 2am, everything came flowing back. The whistling wind still blew through the tall oak trees and, as I closed my eyes, I was instantly transported back in time to the children's home where my twin brother and I spent the first three years of our lives. Although I was only two and a half years old, I still have vivid memories of the day we were split up.

A well-dressed man took John in a car and I was marched down to the station to join the 'orphan train'. The steam from the train masked my tears as I stood on the platform with my belongings—a small brown parcel tied up in string. The old steam train shipped hundreds of children into Glasgow to be dispersed all over Scotland.

Luckily, I was to be blessed with a loving foster family in the Isle Millport who instilled in me a love of people, books, travel, animals and music. Lawrence and Lorraine, my mum and dad, were originally from Aviemore in the Scottish Highlands. They bought the Millport Post Office and over time attached a small coffee shop. Lorraine always wanted a wee boy and when they got the chance they adopted me. I love them both.

Every summer, my dad's friend visited from Glasgow. He was a journalist and went everywhere on his bike. Even though he brought us all presents and was generally upbeat, I sensed a feeling of sadness in his eyes. He bought me a bike and taught me how to fish. "There is more to fishing than fishing," he'd say. Adding, "If you ever get the chance to travel, take it. You will learn a lot more travelling than you ever will in a classroom."

I knew him as Uncle John, the writing, cycling, travelling fisherman. Over the years, I got to know him well and became fond of him.

I never saw him again after my eighteenth birthday party. But what he did was open my eyes to my future.

When it came time to attend university, I said to my parents, "I will travel the world and that will be my education." And so, I did; all over Europe, Asia, Africa, America and Australia. No doubt I'll write about that someday.

On my return, I completed a degree in journalism in Edinburgh with the help of the Oswald study fund set up by my Uncle John. I am now, however, back in Scotstoun tracing my roots and looking for work. Tower blocks have replaced the home where I spent the first two years of my life with my twin brother, John. The six blocks at the Kingsway are occupied mainly by asylum seekers and refugees.

I was lucky enough to get a small studio flat. Paradoxically, I have visited many countries; now I have the world on my doorstep.

The nearby steam train has gone, replaced by an electric line (Electrification was commissioned in 1960 and the L&DR route closed in 1964 except for a short section near Dumbarton. The area is now a cycle track). My plan was to stay for a year and then marry my Australian girlfriend. What is it they say about plans? Last week, I was the happiest and perhaps the poorest writer in Scotland. My girlfriend had sent me a letter saying she wanted to come to Glasgow and spend the rest of her life with me. This seemed too good to be true. It was.

Glasgow is still sick.

The *Glasgow effect* refers to the unexplained poor health and low life expectancy of residents of Glasgow, Scotland, compared to the rest of the United Kingdom and Europe. Though lower income levels are generally associated with poor health and shorter lifespan, the prevailing hypothesis among epidemiologists is that poverty alone does not appear to account for the health disparity found in Glasgow. Equally deprived areas of the UK such as Birmingham, Liverpool, and Manchester have higher life expectancies, and the wealthiest 10% of the Glasgow population have a lower life expectancy than the same group in other cities.

From Wikipedia, the free encyclopaedia

Several hypotheses have been proposed to account for the effect, including vitamin D deficiency, cold winters, higher levels of poverty than the figures suggest, high levels of stress, and social alienation. If we can learn from those who have gone before us, then who knows what the future will bring?

Asier, who was a great nature lover, said this before he passed:

"Another glorious day in which one seems to be dissolved and absorbed and sent pulsing onward we know not where. Life seems neither long nor short, and we take no more heed to save time or make haste than do the trees and stars. This is true freedom, a good practical sort of immortality."

Today, Glasgow still has poor housing services. Compared to Edinburgh, the buses are in Glasgow are dirty and uncomfortable. The National Health Service fails to hook up with internal and external agencies effectively. We must learn what it means to really serve: A system supplying a public need such as transport, communications, health, housing or utilities. And, most of all, we must work together to achieve our goals. Let common sense, wisdom, and compassion prevail.

So, let the healing begin. People must come together to improve their own health and the health of a great city. It's time to place our past troubles in a place we know so well, 'In the Wind', and put the people's needs first.

Spanish Civil War Memorial, Glasgow

Art

Picasso's biographer, John Richardson, turned up the following macabre new insight:

The Market Day Massacre, the historian Xabier Irujo reveals the hitherto unknown fact that the destruction of the historic Basque town of Guernica was planned by Nazi Minister Hermann Göring as a gift for Hitler's birthday, 20 April. Guernica, the parliamentary seat of Biscay province, had not yet been dragged into the Spanish Civil War and was without defences. Logistical problems delayed Göring's master plan. Thus, Hitler's birthday treat had to be postponed until 26 April.

Richardson, also, offers a loose collection of fascinating *Guernica* trivia. He speculates, for instance, that one of the figures in the painting is a portrait of Picasso's lost sister, Conchita. He also recounts a contemporaneous, but more-or-less unrelated episode, where Picasso pointedly rejected the opportunity to shake the hand of Italian Futurist impresario—and Fascist—F. T. Marinetti, by declaring, "You seem to forget that we're at *war*."

During the war, some 30,000 foreigners joined the fight against the fascists, including more than 2,500 Americans. Folk musicians like Tom Glazer did their part back home to spread awareness for the democratic cause. Despite all the art to come out of the conflict, including Pablo Picasso's *Guernica* and Ernest Hemingway's novel, *For Whom the Bell Tolls*, Franco defeated the resistance movement, thanks to the support of Hitler and Mussolini. Yet the music of Glazer and the others has continued to inspire.

"People at that time had a belief that they could change things," Peter says. "It reminds people of how important it is to believe in a cause. It reminds people how important it is to commit yourself to justice, to the possibility for change."

The Way Forward

One student put forward the following having worked at Scotstoun Health and Well-being Centre:

The six principles that aim to give practical support to services as they deliver the *Forward View*'s vision for a new relationship with patients and communities. They require that:

156

1. Care and support is person-centred: personalised, coordinated, and empowering
2. Services are created in partnership with citizens and communities
3. Focus is on equality and narrowing inequalities
4. Carers are identified, supported and involved
5. Voluntary, community and social enterprise and housing sectors are involved as key partners and enablers
6. Volunteering and social action are recognised as key enablers.

These principles underpin successful local activity that improves health outcomes and allocation of resources.

The King's Fund

Writer James Gerard

Like most folk, I have had many 'personal Guernica's' in my life and I have learned a lot from each one. Whilst some things are best left in the wind, some things should be recorded so we can learn from them:

Get it all on record now—get the films, get the witnesses—because somewhere down the track of history some bastard will get up and say that this never happened.
General Dwight D. Eisenhower, on future Holocaust denial

My own personal Guernica came when I was twenty-three years old when I had a complete breakdown. I spent many months on my father's sofa wishing I was dead. I finally moved out and vowed to find out more about depression. I founded a charity called Time Out and found out all I could about mental health. I then went on to write a book called Hope Street Madness Defeated. Finally, I moved from Glasgow to Edinburgh to complete a degree in journalism. It was there, I met my Basque friend, Asier Santamaria, who told me all about the Spanish Civil War. Since then, I have visited him countless times.

The only thing necessary for the triumph of evil is for good men to do nothing.
Edmund Burke

La Pasionara Clyde Place, Glasgow

The figure of Spanish Civil War hero, Dolores Ibarruri (nicknamed the passion flower, or *la Pasionara*), pays tribute to the 534 volunteers from Britain (65 from Glasgow) who lost their lives in the Spanish Civil War.

Erected in 1979 at Custom House Quay, there was fierce opposition from Tory councillors at the time. Sculpted in fibreglass by former shipyard welder-turned-artist, Arthur Dooley (who was so poor, he could not afford the fare from his Liverpool home to see his work erected), it has the inscription: 'Better to die on your feet than live forever on your knees'

It would love to see Glasgow twinned with Guernica before the 100th Anniversary of the bombing of Guernica on 26 April 2037.

It would be great to see the book made into a play or film and an actual peace haven set up in Glasgow.

Also, it was my dream to see Glasgow through the eyes of foreign students; thus, the fictitious notion of 'Haizean Peace Haven' was born. The Mitchell

Library became my second home. Here, I met students from all over the world. As it turned out, meeting and working with these students became my salvation. I also got to listen to their stories and see how they do things in their countries.

Set mainly in war times, the book is principally about family, persevering in a bad situation and serving others. It is part fact, part fiction—faction. The book touches on Scotstoun's proud history.

Whilst I try to imagine, the rattling trams going by my window, the abundance of trees, old-fashioned values, and styles, I am quite aware that I was from a different era.

We can't choose when we are born or when we die, but following the lessons I have learned on this book journey, I am so grateful for everything I have: family, friends, freedom of speech, spirituality, faith, and many forms of love. Having lived here most of my life, I am so proud of the people of Scotstoun, Clydebank, and Scotland. Everyone will have a family member who, against all odds, fought tyranny and evil so we can live in peace today.

People do make Glasgow and they deserve more. The bullying tactics of the Glasgow Housing Association are well known both by the people (we came across scores of examples whilst researching this book) and the legal professions in Glasgow. They will be found out as more people come forward. The problem with most Glaswegians is that they moan about problems but rarely take the matter up with their local councillor, or elected member of parliament. As a result, nothing changes.

A catalyst for change for me was the work of Dr Viktor Frankl.

Logotherapy was developed by neurologist and psychiatrist Dr Viktor Frankl. It is considered the 'third Viennese school of psychotherapy' after Freud's psychoanalysis and Adler's individual psychology. It is a type of existentialist analysis that focuses on a 'will to meaning' as opposed to Adler's Nietzschean doctrine of 'will to power' or Freud's 'will to pleasure'.

Wikipedia

The following list of tenets represents Frankl's basic principles of Logotherapy:

- Life has meaning under all circumstances, even the most miserable ones.
- Our main motivation for living is our will to find meaning in life.

- We have the freedom to find meaning in what we do, and what we experience, or at least in the stand we take when faced with a situation of unchangeable suffering.

His book *Man's Search for Meaning* (first published in 1946) chronicles his experiences as a concentration camp inmate and describes his psychotherapeutic method of finding meaning in all forms of existence, even the most sordid ones, and thus a reason to continue living. He was one of the key figures in existential therapy and was to become my first pebble, guiding me out of the dark.

I am wounded but I will recover in time. And I refuse to feel bad about my city. In my lifetime, the proudest moment I have witnessed, as far as my city goes, was when Glasgow took charge of the Commonwealth Games in 2014. It was as if someone had peppered our dirty old town with fairy dust. Glasgow more than lived up to its friendly reputation and proved to be a warm, generous and enthusiastic host. As the sun shone on the city, the people of Glasgow extended a heartfelt welcome to visitors and roared their support for the athletes who gave their all.

The programme incorporated more women's and para-sport events than ever before, including the debut of Para-Sport Track Cycling, Women's Boxing and the Triathlon Mixed Team Relay. The city had been awoken from a deep sleep and the public sprang into action. The largest ever peacetime volunteer recruitment drive saw 50,811 applications become approximately 12,500 amazing Clyde-siders, and the lowest ever volunteering age cut-off for a major sporting event meant that sixteen-year-olds could take part.

A ground-breaking partnership with UNICEF raised £5 million to help children throughout Scotland and the Commonwealth, with celebrities urging people to text their donations in an emotive and uplifting appeal during the Opening Ceremony. This event alone shows what the people of Glasgow can achieve when they come together as one.

Five years on, two sympathetic housing workers came to my rescue and fixed up my flat. They then left my neighbours and me with a broken drain and a backyard covered in raw sewage for six months. Being on the ground floor, the stench was unbearable. This broke me and I was hospitalised and came close to death (The incident was covered by Glasgow's 'Live' online newspaper).

I will never get over my five-year incarceration; however, I firmly believe that in the end, good will triumph over evil. I will forgive the Glasgow Housing

Association, but I will never forget the treatment I received from Housing Manager Vicki Gara, Housing Manager Robert Jardine, Housing Officer Susan McLeod, and Buildings Manager John Brown. They have a lot to learn about public service and the people who pay their wages.

In spite of everything I still believe that people are really good at heart. I simply can't build up my hopes on a foundation consisting of confusion, misery and death.

Anne Frank

Don't get me wrong, I've had some great times in Scotstoun; obtaining my degree; founding Scotland's first charity for people affected by depression and receiving lots of awards; meeting the Duke of Edinburgh; meeting Glasgow's Lord Provost; travelling with my dad; and being there for my family and friends when needed.

Donating a poppy from the London Tower Exhibition

THE DAY THE WAR ENDED CIVIC RECEPTION
The Rt Hon Lord Provost Councillor Sadie Docherty and Glasgow City
Council together with the Russian Cultural Centre Scotland
request the pleasure of your company at a Civic Reception and commemorative
event Concert
'The Day the War Ended'
to mark the 70th Anniversary of the end of World War II at the City Chambers,
Glasgow
on Saturday 9 May 2015 at 4.00pm.

100th Anniversary of the Bombing of Guernica, 26 April 2037

Other highlights on this journey were visiting Antonio Banderas' bar in Belnamadena, Spain: he played Pablo Picasso in the movie *33 Dias:* and corresponding with Michael Portillo, Stuart Christie, talking to scores of interesting people and researching interesting facts. A massive thanks to all of you.

Stuart Christie

On the last day of July 1964, eighteen-year-old Stuart Christie, born in Partick, Glasgow, departed London for Paris and then on to Madrid on a mission to kill General Francisco Franco. This was to be one of at least 30 attempts on the dictator's life in Spain. Christie hitchhiked into Spain and was arrested in Madrid on 11 August 1964. Before he left England, he was interviewed for a television programme with Malcolm Muggeridge, a known MI6 contact, and asked whether he felt the assassination of Franco would be right. He answered that it would.

When the programme was broadcast after his arrest in Spain, these comments were edited out. Christie faced a military trial and possible execution but was instead ordered to serve twenty years in prison. He served only three years in Carabanchel Prison where he studied for A-Levels and was brought into contact with other anarchist prisoners. Christie was freed on 21 September 1967, thanks to international pressure, with support from notables such as Bertrand Russell and Jean-Paul Sartre. The official reason given by the Franco regime was that it was due to a plea from Christie's mother. Stuart went on to study History and Politics at Queen Mary College, University of London.

George Steer

Journalist, George Steer, told the world the story of Guernica. Despite Francoist efforts to play down the reports, they proliferated and led to widespread international outrage at the time.

A bust of George Steer now stands in Guernica.

Michael Portillo

Former Minister, Michael Portillo, born in Bushey, Hertfordshire, to an exiled Spanish republican father, Luis Gabriel Portillo (1907-1993) and a Scottish mother, Cora (née Blyth) (1919-2014), went on to make a documentary about Pablo Picasso's painting *Guernica*.

John Sawkins. My Five-Year Odyssey

Jim and I had met by chance in Edinburgh, and later down in London, when we were both helping to give our personal insights into matters of mutual psychological interest. We went on to co-write and get published a book, entitled *Hope Street Madness Defeated*. However, keen not to dwell too much on autobiographical material for our next *oeuvre*, we resolved to tackle a totally different topic far removed from our familiar territory.

What followed was a challenge that was to take me personally right out of my comfort zone. I did have a go at fiction previously, but this venture was more of a hybrid kind of *faction*. I knew remarkably little either about the Spanish

Civil War or the Basque nation. Of course, I'd seen Picasso's painting of Guernica, and I'd grown up aware of the continuing presence of Franco in Spain, long after other dictators such as Hitler and Mussolini had been removed from power.

Time to read up on the subject matter, I felt. When you are trawling through the relevant literature on Guernica, you become aware of possible angles you might take yourself. Certainly, I might start with Picasso's mural and how that came about. Alternatively, there was the involvement of Wolfram von Richthofen in the bombing of Guernica. His elder cousin had been famous as the Red Baron, a far more chivalrous gentleman. Then there was the reporting on the war by *The Times* correspondent, George Steer. A little understanding of the politics of the 1930s wouldn't go amiss.

So much for the research for the book. Writing a book is much like a journey. Chance encounters and life events pepper the route. I had started off living in Aberdeen, where my wife, Aileen, was studying for a degree in fine art, but we have recently moved to Edinburgh, where, coincidentally, from the point of view of this book, my wife's painting, *Tree of Guernica,* was exhibited at the Royal Academy of Scotland.

We had holidayed the previous spring in Vitoria and made a day trip to Guernica which was to leave a lasting impression on both of us.

That the oak tree had survived the German bombing was a miracle, but it remains a symbol to this day of the tenacity of Basque culture. Our visit provided factual information from both the local tourist information staff and the gentleman in the souvenir shop from whom I purchased a cherished copy of *Bombas y mentiras sobre Guernica.* Our visit to the Basque Country (Euskadi) was profoundly life-changing for me. As a linguist, I found the language perplexing, but strangely fascinating. Just outside of Vitoria was a huge eco-park, where we spent several hours exploring the flora and fauna of the region.

Of course, you never *just* write a book. During that time, which coincided with my retirement from teaching, I had engaged in a certain amount of voluntary work which involved my contributing to discussions about mental health in the fields of psychiatry, social studies and ethics. The meetings I attended, ostensibly unrelated to the theme of our book, nevertheless helped inform the character of Asier, the Basque doctor, who came to Glasgow in the 1930s.

It is frankly amazing, in retrospect, how many things happen over a five-year period. In Aberdeen, I helped to set up the Blues Jam at the Malt Mill, and now that I am in Edinburgh, I am a co-founder of Mad Jammers Open Mic Edinburgh. I have found performing and participating in music very therapeutic. (Jim will recall my rendition at a pub in Partick of a song I had written fifty years previously!) Equally, I had been an extra in *Utopia*, a film made by Chris Robb et al, from Aberdeen, and I also featured in a training film about psychosis produced by NHS Lothian.

Of course, the real journey has little to do with exploring new vistas: it's more about navigating and/or trawling the deep recesses of our minds. Superficially, we can identify key events and memorable experiences, but it is only when we revisit these by re-reading articles we may have written at the time that we can appreciate their true significance.

I have always found it hard to express feelings about things that have happened to me in a personal capacity, yet I tend to feel more strongly about injustices when I see them delivered to friends or even strangers, and I will willingly bang the drum on their behalf. Reacting emotionally obviously renders us less objective at times, but like a camera zooming in, it allows us to focus on the details.

So, for example, when I raise concerns about the way the Department of Work and Pensions sanctions benefits, it is at the level of the impact of this on the individual. Though I have been involved in collective advocacy, I believe this can sometimes dilute my response, as I seek to find commonality in a variety of experiences. *Weltschmerz* is all well and good, but it lacks the immediacy of the local response, and is ultimately almost devoid of feeling, as such.

Returning to Vitoria only two years after our first visit to Euskadi (The Basque Country) was a delight. Often, attempting to repeat an experience can appear to be tempting fate: will it match up to our anticipation of it? But our week did not in any way disappoint. Donastia (San Sebastian) was stunning; and this time, we viewed it from the other side of town, partly, because the bus deposited us in a new subterranean location.

We found the Spanish bus service excellent, and locating the terminus underground was a great idea. It enabled the passengers to get closer to their destination without creating a potential eyesore in the centre of town. The journey there was much faster this time as we tunnelled through the mountains instead of driving around them.

In Vitoria, too, we discovered many areas of the town that had remained hidden from us on our first trip. We found the ancient sequoia tree, for example, which had been planted way back in the 19th century. Taking our time, we revisited the now familiar eco-park (where it snowed!). And we benefited from the amazing exhibitions of art, both of the classical kind and the abstract variety. We attended the launch of a new exhibition at Artium, only to find ourselves on the front page of *El Correo* the following day!

However, the highlight, and main purpose of our visit, was our trip to Gernika. Obviously, we had taken a multitude of photographs two years earlier, so this time, we dedicated our visit to meeting up with Javier in the Euskal Souvenirs shop, the ladies in the tourist information office, and two more ladies, Iratxe and Idoje, from the peace museum, where multiple events had been scheduled for the week that marked the 80th anniversary of the bombing of Gernika.

Despite being extremely busy on the day, they had been expecting us after continued correspondence with Jim (my co-writer), and not only took photos and copies of our book but also arranged a meeting with Andreas Schaefter from the Peace Research Centre (gernikagogoratuz.org).

Andreas, as I later realised, had had a lot to do with organising the programme for that week. Just picking out a few key events, I noticed that reference had been made, not only to the recent decision by ETA to abandon their armed struggle but also to recent events in Columbia from where a delegation had come to participate on 26 April. George Steer, the British journalist, is remembered for his accurate reporting of events that day (unlike Kim Philby, whom the British government chose to believe because his views seemed more in tune with theirs, i.e., anti-communist!).

Reconciliation was the overwhelming theme this year. This was emphasised by staging works by Franz Liszt at the Church of Santa Maria. There was an attempt to engage young people who might not necessarily know about historical events—such as the dropping of the atomic bombs on Hiroshima and Nagasaki—through the performance of another music concert. The twinning of Gernika with Pforzheim in Germany was enhanced by exhibiting simultaneously work by the Spanish artist, Picasso, alongside work by the German artist, HAP Grieshaber.

The tolling of bells and the sounding of sirens served to remind those gathered in the town about those awful events, now eighty years ago.
Javier, from the souvenir shop, had set me on my journey two years previously when I purchased from him *Bombas I Mentiras sobre Guernica*. I am now re-reading Paul Preston's revised book on the Spanish Civil War. As we noted in

Haizean, stories are constantly changing. We do not see historical 'facts' in the same light over time.

Acknowledgements

I (James) would like to thank Eddie Aitken who helped with our first book *Hope Street Madness Defeated* available at www.amazon.co.uk and my father, James McGinley, who passed away in March 2016. Also, all my family and friends continue to support me. I would like to reserve a special thank you to my Basque university friends, Asier Santamaria and Julio Zurbito who introduced me to the Basque region. Their wives, children, and extended family continue to make me feel welcome when I visit.

My writing partner, John Sawkins, never ceases to amaze me. John, married to artist Aileen, is a gentleman in every sense of the word. And finally, Councillor Lawrence O'Neill who called every week to make sure I was still living, inspired me to keep on writing and even discussed the book with the Japanese Prime Minister when he met him in Hiroshima, Japan.

Though a good deal is too strange to be believed, nothing is too strange to have happened.

Thomas Hardy

Contacts

Gernika Peace Museum Foundation

Foru plaza1.

E 48300 Gernika-Lumo. Bizkaia, Basque Country, Spain

Email: museoa@gernika-lumo.net www.peacemuseumguernica.org

Kids' Guernica is artwork on a global canvas, expressing the spirit of peace and connecting people. More than 160 peace paintings have already been created in 40 countries all over the world.

www.kids-guernica.org

The Hiroshima Peace Memorial Museum is a museum located in Hiroshima Peace Memorial Park in central Hiroshima Japan, dedicated to documenting the atomic bombing that occurred on 6 August 1945.

1-2 Nakajimacho, Naka Ward,

Hiroshima,

730-0811,

Japan

www.pcf.city.hiroshima.jp

The Carnegie Moscow Centre

Established in 1910 by Andrew Carnegie, the Carnegie Endowment for International Peace seeks to advance the cause of peace and draws upon the collective resources of scholars and practitioners located in Carnegie centres in Beijing, Beirut, Brussels, Moscow, New Delhi, and Washington.

16/2 Tverskaya Moscow,

125009 Russia

Phone: +7 495 935-8904

www.carnegie.ru

The Peace Centre
Peace Drive,
Warrington Cheshire
WA5 1HQ Tel: 01925 581 231
Email: info@foundation4peace.org

Holocaust Memorial Museum
100 Raoul Wallenberg Place,
SW Washington, DC 20024-2126
Tel: 202 488 0400
www.ushmm.org

Playing for Change is a multimedia music project, created by the American producer and sound engineer, Mark Johnson, with his Timeless Media Group that seeks to inspire, connect, and bring peace to the world through music. Playing for Change also created a separate non-profit organisation called the Playing for Change Foundation, which builds music schools for children around the world.
info@playingforchange.org

Factual History
For a more in-depth look at Scotstoun's history visit Scotstoun Memories on Facebook. https://www.facebook.com/groups/427274790770597/
Or check out *Old Scotstoun & Whiteinch* by Sandra Malcolm).

Other Books
Bombas y mentiras sobre Guernica, Castor Uriarte Aguirreamalloa, 1976.
Guernica, an epic story of love, family and war, Dave Boling, 2009.
Art Against War: Four Hundred Years of Protest Art Paperback, 1 Dec 1984

By D. J. R. Bruckner (Author), Seymour Chwast (Author), Steven Heller (Author)

A survey of anti-war art features the works of over one hundred artists from many countries, including Breughel, Goya, Manet, Kandinsky, Munch, Sloan, and Searle.

Telegram from Guernica: The Extraordinary Life of George Steer, War Correspondent, Nicholas Rankin, 2013.

On 26 April 1937, in the rubble of the bombed city of Guernica, the world's press scrambled to submit their stories. But one journalist held back and spent an extra day exploring the scene. His report pointed the finger at secret Nazi involvement in the devastating aerial attack. It was the lead story in both *The Times* and the *New York Times,* and became the most controversial dispatch of the Spanish Civil War.

Who was this special correspondent, whose report inspired Picasso's black-and-white painting *Guernica*—the most enduring single image of the 20th century—and earned him a place on the Gestapo Special Wanted List?

George Steer, a twenty-seven-year-old adventurer, was a friend and supporter of the Ethiopian emperor Haile Selassie I. He foresaw and alerted others to the Fascist game plan in Africa and all over Europe; initiated new techniques of propaganda and psychological warfare; saw military action in Ethiopia, Spain, Finland, Libya, Egypt, Madagascar and Burma; married twice and wrote eight books.

Without Steer, the true facts about Guernica's destruction might never have been known. In this exhilarating biography, Nicholas Rankin brilliantly evokes all the passion, excitement and danger of an extraordinary life, right up to Steer's premature death in the jungle on Christmas Day 1944.

About the Book

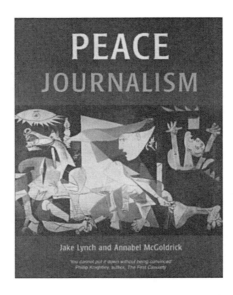

Peace Journalism explains how most coverage of conflict unwittingly fuels further violence and proposes workable options to give peace a chance.

Here are:

- Topical case studies including Iraq and 'the war on terrorism' supported by theory, analysis, archive material and photographs
- A comparison of War Journalism and Peace Journalism
- How the reporting of war, violence and terror can be made more accurate and more useful
- Practical tools and exercises for analysing and reporting the most important war stories of our time

Professional journalists Jake Lynch and Annabel McGoldrick draw on 30 years' experience reporting for the BBC, ITV, Sky News, the London Independent and ABC Australia. They teach Peace Journalism in departments of Journalism, and Peace Studies at several universities. They have led training workshops for editors and reporters in many countries, including the UK, USA, Indonesia, the Philippines, Nepal, the Middle East and the Caucasus.

"Wholly refreshing; it is one of the strengths of this book that a range of problems are raised, from the choice of value-laden words and phrases to broader issues about the underlying ideology of the news agenda, the mindset of journalists working to that agenda and the insidious nature of propaganda. Most importantly, it offers journalists a coherent, practical set of guidelines for facing up to these problems...the undeniable merit of the authors' approach is that it makes journalists think more deeply about their overall responsibilities to society."

From the introduction by Roy Greenslade, Guardian media commentator and Professor of Journalism at City University, London

Guernica 2016 (Movie)

1937 Spain: lines are being drawn, sides are being chosen...and the world will never be the same. As the citizens of the village of Guernica live with the day-to-day realities of the Civil War, an American journalist (James D'Arcy) secretly joins forces with a local press office censor (María Valverde) to work against the stringent restrictions that are becoming more common. But everything changes when German forces attack the town, and the freedom of the press becomes a vital weapon. Based on the historical events of the bombing that set the stage for World War II.

Sedona Art Prize Online 'Make Art Not War'

Furthering our desire to promote peace through art, we're adopting a new slogan, 'Make Art Not War'. A spin-off from the popular 60s term 'make love not war', it's more than a message: it provides a solution for peace, replacing the destructive activity of 'making war' with the creative and unifying activity to 'make art', and share it with the world. Make Art Not War becomes a mantra for people everywhere who envision a world where people come together by sharing a common interest that is creative, unifying, and uplifting.

It is our hope that Make Art Not War spurs an international movement with the goal to provide practical art education to people in developing countries who have no access to art or art supplies, thereby offering them a path out of poverty. Victoria began a similar program two years ago when she lived in Belize. She began an art education program for Belizean children, providing them with art kits and training. The purpose was to eventually help them licence their artwork to provide them with an ongoing stream of income.

So, hopefully, you now understand that to Victoria and me, this is more than just an art contest. It is a vehicle to contribute to a worldwide movement of peace and unity. Make Art, Not War. We will do this by promoting you and your artwork—a powerful message of unity and peace.

Sedona Art Prize
2370 W. SR 89A, Ste 11 Box 200
Sedona, AZ 86336 USA
Email: info@sedonaartprize.com
Phone: 928-282-4326 or 928-201-5082
www.sedonaartprize.com

List of Anti-War Organisations

In order to facilitate organised, determined, and principled opposition to war, peace-centred activists have often founded anti-war organisations. These groups range from temporary coalitions which address one war or pending war, to more permanent structured organisations which work to end the concept of war and the factors which lead to large-scale destructive conflicts. The overwhelming majority do so in a non-violent manner. The following list of anti-war organisations highlights past and present anti-war groups from across the world.

Wikipedia

International

- Christian Peacemaker Teams
- Dartmouth Conferences
- Hands Off the People of Iran
- Institute for Economics and Peace
- International Campaign Against Aggression on Iraq
- International Campaign to Abolish Nuclear Weapons
- International Campaign to Ban Landmines
- International Fellowship of Reconciliation
- International Peace Bureau

- International Physicians for the Prevention of Nuclear War
- Mond paca Esperantist a Movado World Peace Esperanto Movement
- Nobel Women's Initiative organised by female Nobel Peace Prize winners
- Non-violent Peaceforce
- Peace One Day
- Peace Brigades International
- Pugwash Conferences on Science and World Affairs
- Students for Justice in Palestine
- The Nonviolence Project
- War Resisters' International
- World Peace Council
- Women's International League for Peace and Freedom
- World Congress of Intellectuals for Peace

Africa

- Anti-War Coalition
- Committee on South African War Resistance
- End Conscription Campaign
- Koeberg Alert

Asia

- Beheiren
- Peace Now

Europe

- Association de la Paix par le Droit
- Austrian Society of Friends of Peace (German: Österreichische Gesellschaft der Friedensfreunde)
- Centre for Anti-war Action, Serbia
- Dansk Fredsforening, Denmark
- German Peace Society

- Irish Peace Society
- International League of Peace
- League of Peace and Freedom
- Norwegian Peace Association (Norwegian: Norges Fredslag)
- Società per la pace e la giustizia internazionale, Italy
- Societe suisse de la paix, Switzerland
- Soviet Peace Committee, state-controlled organisation during the Soviet Union
- Stop the War Committee, opposed the Second Boer war
- Swedish Peace and Arbitration Society
- Vrede door Recht (Peace through Law), Netherlands

France

- Movement for a Non-violent Alternative (in French)
- Societe Gratry de la paix
- Peace Through Law Association
- Union pacifiste de France (in French)

United Kingdom

- Campaign for Nuclear Disarmament
- Church of England Peace League
- Committee of 100
- Direct Action Committee
- International Voluntary Service
- Liverpool and Birkenhead Women's Peace and Arbitration Association
- Military Families Against the War
- No Conscription Fellowship
- Peace Pledge Union
- Peace Society
- Rationalist Peace Society, Britain
- School Students Against War
- Stop the War Coalition
- Spies for Peace

- Workman's Peace Association, Britain

United States

- America First Committee, opposed American entry into the Second World War
- American League Against War and Fascism
- American Peace Mobilisation
- American Peace Society
- American Women for Peace
- A.N.S.W.E.R.(also known as International ANSWER and ANSWER Coalition)
- Another Mother For Peace
- Anti-War Committee
- Antiwar.com
- Association for Muslims of United States
- Campus Anti-war Network
- Committee for Non-Violent Action (later merged with the War Resisters League)
- Committee for Nonviolent Revolution
- Centre on Conscience & War (formerly known as NISBCO)
- Central Committee for Conscientious Objectors
- Council for a Liveable World
- The Council for National Interest
- Code Pink: Women for Peace
- Common Dreams
- ChildVoice International
- Direct Action to Stop the War
- GI Rights Network
- Gold Star Families for Peace
- Iraq Veterans Against the War
- Iraq Peace Action Coalition
- LewRockwell.com
- Long Island Alliance for Peaceful Alternatives
- Military Families Speak Out, opposed to the war in Iraq

- Moratorium to End the War in Vietnam
- National Campaign for a Peace Tax Fund
- National Coordinating Committee to End the War in Vietnam
- National Mobilisation Committee to End the War in Vietnam
- National War Tax Resistance Coordinating Committee
- New York Peace Society, first peace society in the US, opposed 19th and 20th century wars
- No Conscription League
- Not in Our Name
- Peace Action
- Peace Alliance
- Peace and Freedom Party
- People's Council of America for Democracy and Peace, anti-World War I group
- Port Militarisation Resistance
- Seneca Women's Encampment for a Future of Peace and Justice
- September Eleventh Families for Peaceful Tomorrows
- Spring Mobilisation Committee to End the War in Vietnam
- Students for a Democratic Society (2006 organisation)
- Syracuse Peace Council
- The Buffalo Nine
- The World Can't Wait
- Troops Out Now Coalition
- United for Peace and Justice
- Veterans for Peace
- Vietnam Day Committee
- Vietnam Veterans Against the War
- War Resisters League
- Women Against Military Madness
- Women Strike for Peace
- Women's Peace Party
- Women's Peace Society
- Women's Peace Union
- Youth International Party (Yippies)

Canada

- Canadian Peace Alliance
- Canadian Peace Congress
- Ceasefire Canada
- Nova Scotia Voice of Women
- War Resisters Support Campaign

Oceania

- Global Peace and Justice Auckland
- Peace Action Wellington
- Stop the War Coalition

Religious Organisations
Christian

- American Friends Service Committee
- Anglican Pacifist Fellowship
- Catholic Association for International Peace
- Catholic Worker Movement
- Christian Peace Conference
- Episcopal Peace Fellowship
- Fellowship of Reconciliation
- Friends Committee on National Legislation
- International Catholic Peace League
- Lutheran Peace Fellowship
- Mennonite Central Committee
- Methodist Peace Fellowship
- Order of Maximilian, anti-Vietnam war organisation
- Pax Christi
- Pentecostal Charismatic Peace Fellowship
- Presbyterian Peace Fellowship

Buddhist

- Buddhist Peace Fellowship

See Also:

- List of peace activists
- Anti-nuclear organisations
- Anti-war movement
- Direct action
- Gandhi Peace Award
- Gandhi Peace Prize
- Global Peace Index
- Nobel Peace Prize laureates
- Non-interventionism
- Nonviolence
- Nonviolent resistance
- Nuclear disarmament
- Pacifism
- Parliament Square Peace Campaign
- Peace
- Peace churches
- Resistance movement
- White House Peace Vigil
- World peace

A Basque Festival 2016

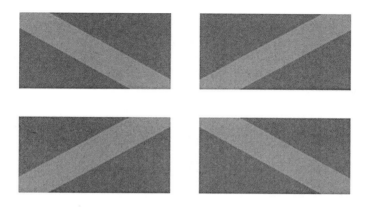

Egoi was a minor divinity among the Basques associated with the south wind.